CARTEL PUBLICATIONS
PRESENTS

BAKE & BAKE
BOYS

A NOVEL BY
MARLO BALTIMORE

Library of Congress Control Number: 2013938001
ISBN 10: 0984993088

ISBN 13: 978-0984993086

Cover Design: Davida Baldwin www.oddballdsgn.com
Editor: Advanced Editorial Services
Graphics: Davida Baldwin
www.thecartelpublications.com
First Edition

Printed in the United States of America

CHECK OUT OTHER TITLES BY THE CARTEL PUBLICATIONS

WWW.THECARTELPUBLICATIONS.COM

What's Poppin' Fam,

As I draft this letter, I have a heavy heart. At the time this book was published, Boston was rocked by the careless acts of two terrorists. For the life of me I do not understand how people can be so cold and heartless. And in a country who embraces people of all backgrounds, ethnicities and religious beliefs. I am a positive person and I try to remain in good spirits, and I'm certain that Boston, and our country will rise and embrace the foundation that the United States was built on...one Nation...under God, indivisible, with liberty and justice for all. I continue to pray for the victims of Boston and their families.

On a brighter note, we bring you to our latest release, "Wake & Bake Boys", by Marlo Baltimore. This story is based on love. Love of two brothers who rely on one another for strength. Love of one brother and his overbearing girlfriend. Love of weed and it's numbing affects on pains from the past. (Laughs) We are certain that Cartel Publications fans will be as proud to add this book to their urban fiction collection, as we are to ours.

Keeping in line with tradition, we want to send love, appreciation and support to the:

Boston Police Department

The Boston Police Department successfully apprehended the second suspect in the Boston Marathon Bombings that took place on April 15, 2013. The Boston Police took the suspect into custody on April 19th alive, and we truly appreciate the tireless efforts they showed in bringing him to justice. They did not rest until they got their man. Well done, Boston PD!

Aight, get to it! I'll see you in the next novel. ;)

Be Easy!

Charisse "C. Wash" Washington
Vice President
The Cartel Publications
www.thecartelpublications.com
www.twitter.com/cartelbooks
www.facebook.com/cartelpublications

PROLOGUE

One Christmas morning, in Washington DC, the heavy smell of weed crept under Dane and Tex's doorway as they slept in their room. When the odor tickled eight-year-old Dane's nose, he stirred a little and sat up in the bottom bunk bed. His feet slapping against the cold wooden floor, and he raised his arms up high.

"It's Christmas," he said with a smile on his ashy face.

Wiping the crust surrounding his green eyes, with his tiny fists, he rose and nudged his brother who was still fast asleep on the top bunk bed.

"Wake up, Tex," Dane said roughly, as he pushed his brother's arm. "Get up, man!"

"Leave me alone." *Seven-year-old Tex pulled the Superman sheet up over his head, and closed his eyes tighter.* "I'm still sleepy."

"But it's Christmas, and daddy's here"— *he continued to poke him*— "I can smell him. Don't you?" *Dane turned around to leave before waiting for his brother's response.*

Playing back the tapes in his mind, Tex thought about what Dane said. Their father whom they hadn't seen in a week was home, and he missed him so much. He couldn't wait to see him, and ask him where he'd been. He threw the sheets off of his body and hopped off of the bed like a grasshopper.

Dane opened the door, and saw their father sitting in the raggedy brown recliner; next to a medium sized half-decorated Christmas tree. Something felt off. Way off. If the blank expression on their father's face didn't hint that trouble was on the horizon for the Blake brothers, the bareness under the Christmas tree all but screamed misfortune. One gift, the size of a small book, was wrapped in green and red paper, with no bow. Nothing else was there.

Dane and Tex's hearts sank to their little feet. The boys weren't strangers to poverty and sorrow. Missing meals, not having new school clothes and fighting the bullies away when they cracked on your tennis shoes was common in the projects, and caused them to rebuild their muscles. But birthdays, and Christmas belonged to the kids and parents struggled to make those days special. So what was up now?

Marvin pulled on the white joint resting between his stubby fingers and waved the boys over. "Come here, I wanna talk to you. Both of you."

They trudged toward him and Dane planted himself at his feet, while Tex sat on his lap.

"Hi, dad," Dane said, offering a smile.

"Hi, son," he cleared is throat. "This is gonna be hard for me, but I figure you're old enough to know the truth. Get that up in you first, you're going to need it." Marvin handed Dane the joint, and he pulled on it slowly, until his developing lungs were filled with polluted smoke. When he was done, he released the clouds from his nose, and handed it to Tex who did the same. Always the weed head, Tex maintained his hold onto the joint for a little longer.

Ever since Marvin Gary had been released from prison six months ago for manslaughter, getting high with his sons was one of the highlights of his day. But now things had changed. Everything changed, and he was having a hard time with the moment.

"Your mother ain't the kind of woman I wanna be with any more," Marvin said to them. "That's why I ain't been around for the past week. And I wanted you to hear it from me, because I need to tell you why."

Tex released the smoke from his lungs, and it brushed against his father's nose. Marvin inhaled the floating smoke and took the joint back.

"Why, what she do?" Tex asked. "Was she mean to you?"

"Your mother's a wretched bitch, of the worst kind," huge tears rolled down his face as he smoked up the rest of the joint. "To kiss a man, and look him in his eyes when you're a liar is vile. I got more

7

respect for the man who killed my mother, than I do for her, and I can't be around here no more."

"Daddy, I'm scared," Dane said looking up into his face with his big green eyes. "I don't like when you talk about mamma like that."

Something evil came over Marvin for a minute as he looked at the boys. He hadn't realized that a seed their mother planted in his heart had grown already, and caused him to hate them both. High and insane, for a second Marvin wished he could pluck the green eyes out of Dane's head. How could he be so blind to think that he was his child? When he looked over at Tex, he had the desire to do the same thing. Still angry, Marvin stood up and pushed Tex off of his knee. He rolled over on the floor and scooted next to his brother.

With the physical connection gone, he reached under the tree and handed Dane the only wrapped gift there. Dane accepted it, and noticed that it was heavier than he imagined it would be.

"You said you were scared, Dane, and I want you to know that being scared ain't gonna do nothing but make you a bitch in life," Marvin told him. "You the oldest, and you gonna have to be a father to your brother, now, because with your mother lost in her mind, you're all you have left." He wiped the sweat off of his forehead. "Don't worry, I had to be a father to my younger brother too when I was 'bout your age. Be better than me though, because my

brother was murdered by a racist white man, for sleeping with his daughter, while I was at the basketball court playing one on one with my friend, and I never forgave myself for letting him down." Marvin stared into the grimness of the two-bedroom apartment. "Never abandon your brother, no matter what."

"But I got a daddy already," Tex said. "I don't need another one. I want you to be my father."

Marvin's forehead creased and his nostrils expanded. "I'm not your fucking father! Don't you see what I'm trying to tell you? Your mother lied, and I'm done with her, and that means I'm done with you too." He hopped off of the recliner, and his body stood over them like the Statue of Liberty. "You'll both get all the answers you need when you open that gift." He grabbed a black leather duffle bag next to the door. "Bye."

Marvin opened the door and a blast of cold air, sprinkled with a few particles of freshly fallen snow, slid inside before he exited their lives for good. Dane tore off the Christmas wrapping covering their gift. When the paper gathered at his feet, and he saw what he was holding, he knew immediately what Marvin was trying to say. They were looking into uncle Larry's eyes, eyes they knew all too well. It wasn't even a new gift, because the photo was taken off of the wall, next to the rest of the pictures in the home including Marvin's.

Since Dane's youngest memory, he recalled Larry being around. On Christmas, New Years, Easter, and every other holiday Larry was always there. Dane observed Larry's green eyes, which were just as bright as his. Then he took in his vanilla colored skin, which was just as light as his. His thin nose didn't mirror his, but it did his brother.

Before he could draw his own conclusion, Diane strolled out of the back, wearing a black robe and no shoes. "He's your father." She looked at the photo in his hand. "I ain't never want ya'll to find out like this, but Marvin felt it was best to tell you now. He caught me stealing a small little kiss, in Larry's car last week, and we didn't want to lie no more, so we told him the truth. We were in love."

"But, I don't understand." Dane stood up and approached her. "Larry not my daddy, he my uncle?" Dane was stuck and wanted more answers. "But how?"

"Don't be ignorant your whole life. I fucked him and he fucked me. I made a mistake two times, and had you kids. It finally came back to haunt me that's all, and now I ain't got no help around here." She ran her fingers through her thick bushy mane. "Now stop whining and get up, and go next door. I got some chicken wings thawing in the sink, but I need some flour and cooking oil to make them right.

I hooked Maumelle up last week when she borrowed two cigarettes, and it's high time she paid me back." She moved for the bedroom door but stopped short before opening it. "And there ain't no need in you wondering when Larry coming back because he ain't. Marvin saw to that too."

Two things happened after that horrendous Christmas day. They would never get to talk to their biological father again, because Marvin shot him in the head while he was playing craps in front of a liquor store. Which eventually would catch up with him, landing him in prison for the rest of his life. The second thing was their mother's health grew worse.

Although it was rumored in the neighborhood that she was bipolar, it became evident when she threw her birthday party and invited everyone to the house for a celebration. But because a character on one of her favorite soap operas died, she threw them out after only fifteen minutes later, to grieve.

Overtime Dane and Tex learned that if they were going to survive, they needed to support each other, and that was exactly what they did. Until...

CHAPTER 1
(Ten Years Later)

Shanti got the prettiest titties I've ever seen in my life. Not too big, not too small, just right. The way she pressing 'em on this counter, while she fills out the paperwork to leave her dog, Rose to be boarded with us, makes 'em look like a sexy ass.

"What you looking at, Dane," she says looking up at me. "Don't eye 'em if you not gonna bite 'em. I'm sick of your fine ass teasing me."

I chuckle. "You going hard now aren't you?"

"No harder than what I normally do. I figure if I keep trying my hand, you'll take the bait."

"That nigga might not be with it, but I am," my brother says. "He can't handle a woman like you. It's too much for him."

He's to my left, and is kissing her dog in the mouth, a gray boxer. Sometimes my little brother goes too far when it comes to the animals. When we were younger he brought in strays on a constant basis...from dogs to rats, no animal was off limits. I think he likes 'em more than he does people.

We work for *Doggy Style Kennel*, in Northwest DC, which is owned by an older man named John Boy who's never here. Me and Tex been working here for about a year, and it's the longest job we ever kept. Mainly because Tex loves animals so he wants to come to work, and since the boss is never here, it gives us space. With a job like this it doesn't feel like work, especially considering we have another hustle that keeps dough in our pockets.

When she's done filling out the emergency contact form, she slides it over to me, and licks her lips. "Ya'll gonna take care of my baby right?" She grabs her dog from Tex, and kisses him in the mouth. What a lucky ass dog. "I don't want to come back and see him all skinny and shit. Make sure you feed 'em, Tex."

"Shanti, don't try and play us," Tex says. "You know ain't nobody in DC takes better care of dogs more than me. I make sure they eat, get they play time in and love. I don't play that bamma shit. That's why the animals don't be wanting to leave when the customers come back to get 'em. I do 'em right." He took Rose from her, and scratched the dog's head.

"You know I'm just talking. If I even thought you would do my Rose wrong, I'd be on your shit, and she wouldn't be here."

"Yeah whatever…we'll see you in a week."

When he walks into the back she asks, "Dane, where you get them sexy green eyes from? Every time I see you and your brother I be thrown off. It ain't too often you see black men with that eye color. What you wear contacts or something?"

My eyes are a sore topic for me, so I want to skate by them every chance I get. They are the only things tying me to my biological father.

"I wear contacts but they're not for color. I'm blind as a bat without 'em."

"I knew your eyes were fake."

"There you go with that dumb shit. My eyes ain't fake, Shanti. I was born with them." I put her form in Rose's file under the counter. "Anyway, what you getting into this week? Why you dropping Rose off?"

Her eyes hang low and she seems mad. "My job sending me to some whack ass sales convention in New York. Like I'm gonna sell more eye shadow than I already do now. I'm getting real tired of that job. It's so stupid."

"What you tripping for? The way I see it you got an expense paid trip. If anything you should go, do the work thing for an hour, leave early and enjoy the city. When you leaving?"

She looks at the gold Bulova on her arm. "I'm going to Regan airport now, and I'm mad about that shit too. Out of all of the airports in the DMV (DC,

Maryland and Virginia), they would send me through that one." She sighs. "Anyway, I know what would make my trip real nice, if you packed a bag and came with me." She rubs my hands. "You wouldn't have to pay for shit, Dane, I swear to god."

"I wish I could, ma. But I'm stuck out here, I got something to do later."

She frowns, and takes her hand back. "Let me guess, it's because of your little girlfriend Asia isn't it?" she rolls her eyes. "I wish you dump that chick and get with a real bitch, Dane. She can't be fucking you right." She runs her hand through my short curly hair. "With your sexy ass self."

"Asia does me just right in the bedroom, Shanti. And anything I do decide to do on the side with you, won't concern her."

"Why are you so serious about her? Whenever I ask about her you get mad. You're in love ain't you?"

"Didn't I say that's my personal business?"

See that's the shit I hate 'bout bitches sometimes. Instead of enjoying whatever we got going on, they like to bring my girlfriend's name up. I don't care how bad a bitch is, or how good she fucks, they will never make me leave Asia.

While Shanti is a cutie on the outside, Asia's a total package. She's sexy, smart, and proves over and over again that she's down for me. If I ever do settle down, which I'm not even thinking about right now, she gonna be the one.

"One of these days I'm gonna get some of that dick, and you gonna fall in love with me too."

"Maybe I'll take you up on that offer," I wink. "One day."

After she paid her bill and left, I turn on the TV. In an hour we will be closing. I lock the door, even though we're not supposed to shut down until forty-five minutes to eight o'clock. John Boy doesn't know it, but nobody comes in at this hour so it's cool. When the show *Jeopardy* comes on, I position myself in front of the counter ready to go.

"I'll take populous nation for $400.00," the contestant says.

Alex says, *"Israel, Lebanon, Syria."*

"What is Syria," I say before the woman can answer.

"What is Israel," the contestant says and gets it wrong.

When the next person says my answer, and is correct, I slap the counter. "I knew that shit! That was so fucking easy! How did you get that wrong?" I yell to the TV.

"Populous Nation for $600.00," the winner says.

"Switzerland, Sweden, Swaziland," Alex says.

"What is Sweden," I say before he can.

16

When the contestant says my answer and is correct I cheer. "They need to get me on that show. I'll fucking kill them."

While I'm looking at the show my brother comes out the back wearing his red Chicago Bulls cap to the back. Although we got the same father, he's 5'5 with a baldhead, and I'm 6 feet even, with curly black hair, and I always wondered how that happened. The only thing that's the same on us are our green eyes, and since my mother don't have them, I figure they must've come from our father.

"Fuck you out here making so much noise for?" He bounces and catches a small red ball that he always played with wherever he goes. I don't know where he gets them, but they look like the ones that come out of a box of jacks. "You gonna excite the dogs, and get 'em all riled up before we leave."

"Ain't nobody riling up no fucking dogs. Did you feed them," I ask, still looking at the TV. "We about to leave in a minute."

"You know I got them dogs, and what's up with you and that Jeopardy shit?" He looks at the TV. "Knowing that kind of shit don't get niggas paid, I thought you knew that already."

"Do you realize how dumb you sound? No seriously, don't say no more ignorant shit like that around me, unless you want to get punched in the face." I pause. "Anyway, you ready?"

"Yeah, I got a bag of blaze from Derrick out southwest in the back," he says to me. "You trying to fire up in the bathroom before we leave?"

"Naw, let's wait until we get out in the car. Samantha said something to Wayne the last time we did that shit, and we almost lost our jobs. You remember when he kept trying to convince us that the dogs caught a contact, and were acting different when their owners came to get 'em?"

"Yeah, aight. Samantha a hating ass bitch anyway, but I'll wait if you can."

When Samantha gets there, I walk out back towards the car we share, a money green 1965 Mustang Fastback, with a Cammer engine. Painted on the side is a weed plant, outlined in gold, which was Tex's idea. We call it the *Weed Mobile*. I admit, we could've been a little more original on the name but whatever.

When I slide inside the car, and rest on the butter cream seats, I pull out my after work blunt and fire up. The moment I take my first pull, and hold it in my lungs, I can feel the muscles in my face and body loosen up. When I can't hold it anymore, I release the smoke into the car, and breathe it back in through my nose.

Five minutes later, Tex bops toward the car and slides into the driver's seat. "Damn, nigga, what took you so long?" I ask him.

"You know I had to make sure Samantha knows what's going on for the night. Plus Rose was sneezing a lot a minute ago, and she's gonna need her meds in about an hour."

"Let me find out you an old Nurse Betty type nigga when it comes to dogs," I laugh. "Now that you done with the dumb shit, are you ready to get down to business?"

He pulls out his after work blunt and fires up. "Yeah, when she say she heading to New York?"

"Now, so let's head over there, and clean that bitch out."

CHAPTER 2

TEX

I'm behind my brother, while he picks the lock to Shanti's house. I'm carrying a black plastic trash bag, and we're both wearing latex gloves. There's something that comes over me when we're about to hit a house. I get a rush that makes my dick hard, and finding things of value only intensifies my high. Once we are inside, I'm surprised at how messy her house is. There are dishes on the stove, caked up with food and it smells like she hasn't taken the trash out in weeks. A nasty bitch.

"I knew something was up with that chick," I tell Dane. "It's a good thing you ain't fuck her."

"Stay focused, we don't know who saw us coming in here." I walk down the hallway toward the back. "Let's go to the bedroom." Once we were inside he was on his regular bossy shit. "Fuck you looking all crazy for? Standing over there next to the mirror. Check up under the bed, and make yourself useful."

"Why you get to check the dressers and shit?"

"Because her shoes might get us paid too. She had on a pair of Christian Louboutins, and I know we can sell them for a hundred even around the way. Now hurry up and stop asking dumb ass questions. Somebody could've seen us."

"How come you always do that shit," I ask holding two different shoes in my hand.

"Do what shit?" He's looking through her drawers.

"Talk to me like I'm a kid?"

"Not this shit again," he sighs. "Listen, just look up under the bed and see if she got any label shoes we can sell. Any other time I could address your feelings but right now is not the time, lil bro. Get busy."

The nigga is trying to play me. "You know what, fuck this shit"— I sit on the edge of the bed and light the bar I rolled in the car— "if you want to see if she got shoes with labels on 'em, you look for yourself." I pull and blow the smoke into the air. I feel better already. "I ain't your fucking slave."

"Nigga, are you seriously smoking in this bitch's house? And leaving evidence?"

"You see me don't you?"

"You doing this shit at the wrong time." He drops to his knees, and looks up under the bed. Before I know it a red and gold shoe comes flying in my direction. I duck before they knock me in the head. "Just put them in the fucking trash bag, and stop fucking around."

"Why I gotta do it? You got hands too."

"What the fuck is up with you," he says to me. "Are you on your period or something? Because I swear you acting like a female right now."

"Ain't nothing wrong with me," I pull on the bar again. "I just don't feel like being bossed around that's all."

"Tex, if you don't put them shoes in that bag in your hand, I swear to God I'm gonna climb over there and fracture your jaw. I'm not fucking around with you now."

He looks at me for five seconds, and I smash the bar out on the dresser, before sticking the un-used portion in my pocket. Then I toss the shoes in-to the trash bag. It's not that I'm scared of my brother or nothing; I just don't feel like being up in here fighting with him that's all. Plus I got a lot of shit on my mind, that I want to tell him about, but I'm not sure how he will handle it.

I met this girl name Juicy up at the flea market in Baltimore last month, when I rolled with Dane to meet this chick Memory that he fucked on the side. His side bitch had a stand in the market where she sold dumb shit like colorful socks, and hats. Stupid shit. Anyway, the only thing I was interested in when we got to the market was her best friend Juicy, who had an ass the size of a beach ball, and I'm not even playing.

One thing led to another, and before I knew it I was breaking this girl's back out in the backseat of the Weed Mobile. The thing was I didn't wear a condom, and now I had some strange bumpy shit on my dick, that wouldn't go away. And every time I showered and looked at it, it made me want to find that slut and choke her ass out. I got an appointment tomorrow to take care of it.

I'm going through her closet when my brother calls me. "Aye, Tex, look at this shit, she got five hundred dollars in her panty drawer."

I walk over to him, and snatch the stack out of his hand. "I love when they leave shit in the house instead of the bank." I take my cut before we get to the car, and hand him the rest. "I wonder what else she got in here." When I look in one of the other drawers, I see a white iPhone. "What about these, we can sell them too."

"Naw, we not fucking with no phones."

"Why not? We can make money off of these mothafuckas. Luke from Southwest be recycling these joints and selling them to dope boys. We can get at least a bill."

"We not selling them because they got serial numbers on 'em, and if they investigate this rob-bery, and somebody activates the phone, whoever we sold it to won't have no problem snitching on us to avoid robbery charges. Now bag that jewelry up over there and let's rock."

Sometimes I hate this nigga!

After the robbery, we sold everything we had to a couple of niggas around the way. In the end with the $250.00 and the things we sold for cash, we had about $750 a piece. That's a good night but we've done better in the past.

We sitting in the car, in front of the playground smoking the blaze. It's so cloudy in here, I can barely see my brother's face, and my eyes are dry. Feeling good, I decide to tell him about my little problem. "I wanna rap to you about something, but I don't want you looking at me the wrong way. Like I'm some faggy or something. It's just that I never dealt with no shit like this before."

He looks over at me, shakes his head and laughs. "Tex, you acting like we not brothers." His eyes are red. "If ever there's anything on your mind, know that you can come to me about it. That's what I'm here for. I mean we fight but it don't have nothing to do with our bond."

I exhale, pass him the blunt and say, "It's like this...I—"

I hear a small buzzing noise. "Hold on, Tex, my phone going off." He takes it out of his pocket and looks at the screen. "It's Asia, let me see what she want. Hold that thought though."

I can't fucking stand that bitch! Since the moment Dane met her in 9th grade, she been on the nigga's dick, and ain't been nothing but trouble. If we go out to eat, she gotta go with us. If we go bowling, she gotta go with us. If he gotta go to the bathroom, she gotta hold his dick. This bitch is worrisome, and I want her dead. There hasn't been a day that goes by that I don't think how better the world would be if she wasn't in the picture.

While he raps to her on the phone, I fire up another blunt. I try not to listen to his phone call, but she just burns me the wrong way.

"Naw, I'll be home when I can, babes."

This bitch acts like she lives with us or something. Or she's his wife. What's up with that shit?

"You know I just got off of work, Asia." He pauses. "Just kicking it with my brother." He pauses again and looks over at me. "I just said I don't know what time I'll be home, baby."

He reaches for the blunt but I don't hand it to him. I ain't sponsoring his dumb ass conversations; with a sack I bought myself. Fuck that shit. When he steals me in my arm real hard, I hand it over to him anyway.

"Aight, baby, I gotta go"— you know I do."
He pulls on the blunt, and releases the smoke into
the car. "Why you want to hear me say it? You already know how I feel."

You see what I'm saying? Whenever he
around me, she always wants to make him say he
loves her, like we fucking or something. I think she
believes that I encourage Dane to dip into chicks on
the side, but he do that shit on his own. Dane loves
pussy more than he loves weed, and there ain't no
way he'll settle down with her, I don't care how
good her sex is.

When he has my blunt too long, I snatch it out
of his hand. I lean back into my seat and think about
what I'm gonna get into tonight. I already called
Bird, my girl's best friend to see if she wanted to
fuck. I been trying to get at her for a minute, but she
would never bite. She'd flirt with me and that was
the extent of it, but I can still feel she likes me.

I'm pulling on the bar again, when a baseball
bat crashes into the driver side window.

CHAPTER 3

DANE

The sky is dark, and I'm sitting on the hood of our car with my two-year old nephew Logan. It's 10:00 o'clock at night, and he out here as usual with no shoes or clothes on. That ain't even the half. The real blower is that Ray-Ray, his mother, is in the middle of the street, trying to fight my brother.

Why Tex fucks with that dumb bitch is beyond me. She crashed our driver's side window just now, over some bitch he supposedly fuck. I was about to choke her out myself since the car was half mine, but I left him to handle the shit on his own.

"You good little, man?" I ask my nephew.

"Yes," he nods, before pushing his index finger into his diaper. I guess he needs changing.

"You got a lot going on in there don't you?"

Yes. It's heavy." Logan scratches his wild curly black hair with one hand, while he rubs the puffiness of his diaper with the other.

I'm still looking at my nephew when shit gets wilder in the middle of the street. "Why the fuck you calling my friend, Bird on the phone, Tex," Ray-Ray says to him. "What the fuck is up with you?"

She's wearing a pair of tight blue jean shorts that showcases one of her lopsided ass cheeks. She claimed she didn't get no botched ass job, but I think she too embarrassed to tell the truth.

"You sound stupid as shit," Tex yells. Both of them move out of the way of a passing car, before going back into the middle of the street.

"It ain't stupid, Tex. You know how fucking embarrassing it is to have your friend call you, and tell you your man trying to fuck her?"

Tex wipes his hands down his face. "Ray, I can't believe you out here in the middle of the street trying to fight me over this shit. And then you had the nerve to crash my car window. Don't you realize nigga's get killed for less?"

"Fuck that dumb ass car ya'll driving around in. I don't' give a fuck about it or you!"

"Why you gonna make me crack you in your jaw in front of my son? Why you gonna make me do that, huh?"

Ray-Ray stands on guard like a man, raises her hands in the air, and swings in his direction. She catches Tex with a firm blow to the cheek, which she follows up with a punch to his chin. Tex, grabs

28

both of her wrists, and tosses her against a broken down ice cream truck. Her head slams against the hubcap of the wheel, and she rubs the back of her natural bush.

"I'm gonna kick your ass now," Ray-Ray promises hopping up. "I'm gonna beat your ass like you a bitch. It's gonna be so good my son gonna start calling me daddy."

Tex ain't the best nigga in the world, he ain't even nice, but when it comes to his son he loves him the best way he knows how, and he doesn't like comments about his fatherhood being questioned by anyone...including his mother.

My brother takes one look at me, and I grab Logan off of the hood of the car, and carry him toward the corner store. I don't know what he is about to do to Ray-Ray, but the look in his eyes told me he didn't want his son watching.

"You want some ice cream, little man?"

"Yes"— he opens the palm of his hand— "I want this much."

"You got that."

"I love you uncle, Dane," he says grabbing my face with his gritty little hands, and kissing me on the nose. "You love me too?"

"You know I do, Logan." I open the corner store's door, and a blast of cool air rolls over my face. It's freezing in here. I hope he doesn't catch a cold since his mother is too trifling to put a shirt on him. "You the coolest nephew in the whole world. I told you that."

I don't know where Logan came from, but despite his evil mother, he is always giving love. Hugs, kisses, smiles, he does all he can to show the people he likes that he cares about them. Just a kid with a lot of charisma, but wild ass parents. A charming type nigga.

I buy him a red push pop, which is a bad idea because already he got sticky shit on the collar of my shirt, and a Pepsi for me with a bag of Doritos stuffed with cheese and meat sauce...my favorite. When we make it back to the car, Ray-Ray is leaning up against the side of it, with Tex in front of her slobbing her down. These mothafuckas kill me.

"I don't care if ya'll back together or not, Ray, you gonna pay for our window," I tell her, handing her Logan, who is dripping ice cream all over her shorts.

"Shut up, boy." She places Logan on her hips and he doesn't move. "I already gave Tex the two hundred dollars he told me it may cost. So don't even come at me like that."

"What got into you?"

"Your brother that's what." She sighs. "But for real, I was wrong for fucking your car up and I'm sorry. I don't want you looking at me all funny and shit when I come back to your house."

"How come you do ghetto shit like that, and then apologize for it later," I ask, sitting on the hood. "You know you mothafuckas can't stay away from each other for long. And now you out two hundred dollars. It was a waste of time."

She shrugs. "Fuck all that. I went off because Tex gonna make me kill one of these bitches out here. At first I thought Bird was lying when she said he called her, and was trying to get at her like that. Now I don't know."

"She was lying," my brother says, taking Logan off of her hip. He sits him on the hood of the car next to me. "I'm not trying to fuck that girl."

"Then what you called her about?"

"Wasn't nobody fucking that bitch. I was calling that girl to see if you was at her spot, and to find out where my son at. Why would I want her, when I got you? Ain't nobody thinking 'bout that fat bitch."

"Then how come whenever you high, you be asking me for a three way with her? If she fat that should be the last thing you should be thinking about."

"When I'm high I want a lot of shit, Ray. Plus I asked you because I really wanted to see if you loved me enough to do whatever I ask." He licks Logan's ice cream, because he keeps trying to share it with him. "I guess I was wrong."

"You nigga's is crazy." I say. "But look, you got another bar on you?"

"I'm out, bro. As a matter of fact I need to get a pack right now." He looks up the street and flags down Wico, a Spanish chick with a bop harder than any dude I've ever met.

Wico rocks up the street with her oversized jeans scratching against the city's ground. She daps me up and then my brother.

"What up, Ray?"

"Wico," she responds rolling her eyes.

The streets have it that one time Ray-Ray was crushing on Wico. But when Wico cracked on her shape, she took to slamming her about being gay every time she saw her.

"What you need," Wico asks Tex. She tugs at the crotch of her jeans like something is there.

"What you working with tonight?"

"Shit...you know all I do is the blacks, so my shit stay potent. I got Black Ganja, Black Bart, Black Gold and my partner up the street just got a hold of some Black Grunion. But if you want that I gotta flag him down here, because I don't have none on me."

"Naw you good. Let me see the Black Bart, I think that's what I had last time. It's dark over here though." He looks back at me. "Aye, Dane, let me see your phone."

I walk over to him and turn on the flashlight. Wico digs into her pocket and pulls out a nickel bag. It's so common to make drug transactions out here that nobody's scared of getting locked up. I shine my light on it, and Tex opens the bag and smells it. When I see him frown I already know something is off. He places his fingers inside of it, and I can see from here that the weed crumbles.

"Wico, why the fuck you trying to play me, son? You know this pack some bullshit."

"What you mean, Tex?"

"Nigga, for starters it's dry...I mean what the fuck I'ma do with this? Plus what's up with all the sticks and seeds? Get the fuck out of here with that shit before I crack you."

"My bad, Tex, that pack was for somebody else." She sticks it back into her pocket.

"You shouldn't be giving that shit to nobody, son. Now let me see what I asked for, before I fuck you up out here."

"No need to get hostile, my nigga," she says raising her hands. "I got you." She dips into her other pocket and pulls out another bag. "What you think 'bout this? This ain't no bullshit."

"Let me check it, Tex. You hold the phone." When he shines the light on the pack, I open the bag and the odor is so strong my mouth waters. I grab some between my fingers, and can see that it has little hairs on it. It's also extra sticky, just like we love it. I even see crystals. This is grade 'A' shit I know it!

"We good with this"— I hand Wico the pack back— "how much you got on you?"

She grins. "How much you need?"

"Give me a 'O'."

"Cool, for that amount, I'll throw in some blunts too."

"Throw in that nickel too, and we sweet."

"Bet," she says rolling her eyes.

She runs up the street and then comes back with the pack.

After we give her the one hundred dollars, Tex says, "Hey, before you leave, we got some Christian Lou's them bitches be wearing in the trunk. They red and only been worn once. You trying to buy 'em?"

Wico looks at her sneaks "Fuck outta here with that dumb shit. You know I don't wear no female shoes. I'll holla at you later, unless you insult me again."

Tex laughs. "Real quick, let me wrap to you 'bout something before you slide off." He looks back at me and they go out of earshot. I wonder what they're talking about, but I don't sweat it.

"What was that about?" I ask when Wico leaves and Tex comes back.

"Nothing for you to worry 'bout."

I shake my head. "Anyway, you's a silly ass nigga for asking that girl if she wanted to buy some high heels."

"She still a bitch." He shrugs. "How I know she wouldn't throw them joints on?"

Tex snapped a picture holding the weed by the car. I took one with him too, but made him put the 'O' down.

We roll up a blunt, and when I see Ray-Ray puckering her lips like she's ready to share it with us, I roll up another one for myself. I don't smoke behind her, she too nasty for me.

We leaning on the car, talking shit and playing with Logan. I'm about to grab something to eat until I see my brother about to pass my nephew the bar to smoke. I punched Tex dead in his chest. "Don't do that shit, son. He a kid."

"Why...he ain't a fetus. His lungs already built," he says to me.

I frown. "You been letting him blaze? Is you crazy, nigga? Fuck wrong with you? You can kill him like that. What you want him to be fucked up like us? To the point where he'll always be needing it?"

"Dad, use to do it to us, and we fine," he shrugs. "What's the problem?"

"Well that mothafucka wasn't our pops, so he ain't give a fuck about us. Remember he rolled out on us on Christmas day. But this little nigga right here is our blood"— I point at Tex— "and we can't do him like that. Aight?"

"Man, ain't nobody—"

"Nigga, you hear what the fuck I'm saying," I yell. "Be a better dad than that nigga was. This ain't some fucking doll, he's your son, and my nephew. And if I ever find out you doing this shit again"— I look at Ray-Ray— "either one of you, you gonna have me to deal with."

"Aight, man, whatever," he says under his breath. "Chill the fuck out, you killing my vibe and my high."

Tex looks over at Ray-Ray, I guess to see if she's looking or not. I didn't mean to play him like that in front of his girl, but we already fucked up due to the damage Marvin caused us from smoking at an early age.

We can't start our day without smoking. We can't fuck without smoking. If we about to get something to eat, we gotta smoke first. And don't let us go for more than four hours without getting high, we be on some evil type shit all day. This habit is serious. This shit has impacted us more than I wanted it to, and I don't want that for my nephew.

I'm just about to eat my soggy Doritos when my phone gets a text message. When I look down I see it's from my girlfriend Asia. Fuck! I forgot she was supposed to be coming over my crib later on. I hit the button to read her message.

U need 2 come home now. I've been waiting on U all day at your house. Stop fucking around, Dane. It's important!

CHAPTER 4

DANE

Because Asia was mad at me for meeting her at my house late, I'm on my knees with my tongue running across her slippery clit. Asia is the only girl I met who loved her pussy eaten so much, she cries when I don't do it for her. I'm talking about she'll cut me off for days if I refuse, or if I bust a nut early without hooking her up.

"Mmmmm…just like that, baby." Asia moans. "Make it wet, baby." I put a little spit on it. "Wetter, Dane! Stop fucking around down there before I fuck you up. I'm talking Niagara Falls!"

My dick is rock hard due to the way she's talking to me. She acts like a maniac when I don't do it the way she wants, and that's part of the reason I love her. Outside of being smart as shit, and sexier than any bitch I ever fucked with in my life, Asia's gonna tell you what's on her mind. She knows who she is, and she definitely knows what she likes to feel.

My fingers press into her chocolate thighs as I put everything but my hair in her pussy. She's tugging at my curly hair, and talking shit at the same time. I'm holding my breath like I'm under water and I'm good at it.

"Yeah, just like that, eat that pussy you red mothafucka. Lick it real good. Mmmmmm. Mmmmmmm. Yeah…you better not stop, you hear me? I'ma fuck you up if you stop, Dane…oh yeah…just like that…kill it with the B, baby. Kill it with the B!"

I have no idea what *kill it with the B* is, but I know the last time I stopped licking her box to ask, she got so mad she left and ain't talk to me for a week.

When I see she's getting oilier, I start flicking my tongue over her button faster until she's grabbing my hair so hard, I open my eyes and look for the Tylenol, because I'ma need it when she's done. When her thighs tighten up, then her legs stretch out, and she screams out my name, I know I've done my job.

"Oh…Dane, I love you so much, Dane….I'm cumming…I'm cumming. Yes, baby, yes!"

I tear my face from between her legs, lick my lips and say, "You good now?"

"I think that was the best you've ever done it.

"You say that all the time." I push her back onto the bed, face up and pull my pants down. "Now it's time for you to return the favor. Fuck the compliments."

I stroke my dick a few times and slide into her soaked pussy. That's the best part about eating her out, before we go at it. The pussy be so warm and so wet, not fucking it would be a waste of a good box. It would be like Barbequing a steak and not eating it.

I grip her ass cheeks, and pound into her roughly. As I'm fucking her I look down at her pretty face. She's moaning and that ain't doing nothing but making me stiffer. Asia has the complexion of a Hershey's Chocolate candy bar, real dark and real pretty. Her nose is small, and matches her face perfectly. She resembles a black Barbie. There's nothing about her that I don't like.

My chest presses against her small breasts and she bites down on her lips. I fucking love this girl. It's to the point where if we beefing, even if I don't let her know, it fucks with my mind.

Although everything else on her is small, that doesn't include her ass. It's so fat that a month back I bet her I could put a saucer on that joint and it wouldn't fall off. I won fifty dollars that night.

"I'm about to cum, baby, keep moving," I tell her. "Don't stop." When I feel my body warm up, I splash my cum into her pussy, and kiss her softly on

40

the lips. "Damn that shit was right tonight," I say. "Why your shit be so good, A?"

"Because we been fucking since we were thirteen. We pros at this shit now. If we were in the Olympics they would make us stars. Gold medals and all."

"There you go"— I laugh— "Always talking shit." I pull my dick out of her and lay next to her on my bed. "Now when you gonna kick shit real to me? You never let me bust off in you unless you want something, did something or got bad news." I stroke her long black hair. "So which is it?"

"Why it gotta be bad?"

"I'm not saying that it's bad but I know something is up. Normally you be all like, *'don't cum inside of me, Dane or I'ma fuck you up. I'm serious, boy'*. Why you ain't give me all that today?"

She looks into my eyes. "Because I do gotta tell you something." She swallows. "I'm leaving DC, baby."

My heart thumps, and I sit straight up in the bed. I grab a fist full of my white sheet and cover my dick. I look at the poster on my wall of Lebron James. "You playing right?"

"No." she says softly. "I'm serious, and I never been more serious in all of my life."

I turn around to look at her. "So...uh...where you going? And when?"

She smiles a little and for a second I feel like hurting her. The last thing I need her to do right now is play with my mind. Instead of answering me, she hops out of bed and jogs toward her brown leather purse on my dresser. It's next to all of the academic trophies I've won in my lifetime. School is so easy for me, that I usually get put out for not paying attention. But every time they test me, and I get perfect scores, they think I'm cheating. It's almost like I can't win or lose.

Her ass jiggles as she digs around inside her purse and I want to lick that clit and start all over again, until I remember what she just said. That she's going to leave me. It takes a minute but eventually she grabs two pieces of paper out of her bag, runs over toward the bed and hops on it.

"Take it," she says trying to hand me one of the papers.

I look down at them. "What is it?"

"Dane, please just look at them."

I take it out of her hand and read over everything really quickly. Before long I understand perfectly what's going on. It says she has received a full scholarship to Prairie View A&M University. In Texas, miles away from DC.

"They accepted me, baby," she smiles. "They accepted me and I'm going." Her smile widens. "Aren't you happy for me? All of the hard work finally paid off, and I get to do what I always wanted, be a lawyer."

I slink out of bed, jump into my jeans (no boxers), and grab my weed on the dresser. "Yeah...why wouldn't I be happy for you?" My back is faced in her direction. "You my baby. You know that."

I don't want her to see the sour look on my face. I know I'm probably playing myself off like a sucker, but she didn't prepare me for this shit. We're together almost everyday and not once did she tell me she was going to college. Or where she was applying. Maybe we weren't as close as I thought we were.

You gotta understand, me and Asia are together all the time. She ain't just my bitch. Outside of my brother, she's my best friend. To not see her pretty face everyday is gonna fuck me up, but still, I want the best for her. *I think.*

I can hear her breathing heavily behind me. She's worried. *What the fuck kind of nigga are you?* I say to myself. *To upset your girl when her only crime was loving you?*

So I pull myself together, get rid of the jealousy on my face that might hold her back from having a real chance at life. And when I'm good, I turn around and face her. Her expression is stuck, like she needs me to be excited, before she can celebrate her accomplishment. I take a fresh bar over to the bed, neatly rolled and stuffed. I sit next to her and fire it up.

"Are you sure you happy for me," she asks, rubbing my back. "Because it don't feel like it."

I pull on the bar and release the smoke into the air. "Asia, you the smartest person I know. I've seen you run rings around niggas in class."

"You crazy"— she nudges my arm— "you run rings around me in Jeopardy all the time. And you the only person I know who is never at school but gets straight A's."

"Come on, baby. I ain't talking 'bout me right now; I'm talking 'bout you. Nobody is smarter than you, and on top of all of that shit, you a good person. When I say I want this for you, I need for you to believe me. You deserve happiness. And if you don't take that scholarship, when you got a chance to get out of fucked up ass DC, you'd be a fool."

"You gonna miss me?"

My heart thumps. She really is about to leave me. "What you think?" I take another pull and hand it to her. "I'm done when you get on that plane, you know that."

"What about you? Do you deserve happiness?" She pulls, and keeps the bar longer than I want her too. That's her only weakness, holding onto the smoke longer than the regulated unofficial timeframe. "I'm not the only one who does great in school, Dane. If I deserve this chance you do too."

44

"Fuck yeah I deserve happiness." I snatch the smoke from her.

She reaches behind her and hands me the second paper. "Good, because I applied for your scholarship also, and you were accepted, Dane. With me. Looks like we're both going to get out of the hood. That means you going with me too. Happy now?"

CHAPTER 5

DANE

I'm looking at her wide eyes, and the excitement etched all over her face. She wants this for me so badly, but I wonder what is her real reason. What's her motive? Sometimes I think Asia just does shit to keep and eye on me.

"How did you do this?" I look down at my scholarship acceptance letter, which I didn't apply for. "I mean…I don't understand. You ain't tell me nothing 'bout this."

"I clean your room every weekend, Dane. I throw out your trash, cook your food when I'm not at work, and spend so much time over here, I should be paying rent. You know I hate to be in my house alone, ever since my mother died. I feel more at home here."

Asia's mother died in a freak accident last summer. She was coming out of her job, at the phone company, and slipped on the icy stairs out-

side. She broke her neck and back and died instant-
ly.

"Well what about my information?"

"Like what," she giggles. "Your social? Boy, I
know your social security number from front to
back. You are my everything and I am yours." She
rubs her hand over my cheek. "We are interconnect-
ed, so why wouldn't I be able to fill out an applica-
tion for a scholarship for you? And answer every
question without your help? That's light weight,
Dane."

"So how did you know it would be here?"

"I check your mailbox everyday. Your mother,
God bless her heart, ain't right in the head, and the
only thing Tex cares about is getting high. Wasn't
nobody but me worried about that mailbox outside.
Trust me. It's right on the curb in front of your
house, and it doesn't have a lock. It was easy."

"Wow..."

"Dane"— she rubs my leg— "aren't you happy? This is a dream come true for the both of us. We
can be in college together, learn together, and more
than anything, still have our relationship. I don't
want to go to the next step of my life without you,
baby. So please don't make me."

"Asia, how I know you not doing this shit to
keep an eye on me? It ain't like you don't be sweat-
ing me about—"

Asia slaps me so hard in the face I lose focus.

I look directly into her eyes. "What I tell you about that shit?" I frown. "Didn't I tell you if you ever did that shit again, I would leave you?"

"I'm...I'm sorry...I just—"

"Didn't I tell you it would be over, Asia?" I yell.

"Yes."

"Then why you keep doing that fucking shit?" I stand up and move away from her, because I feel violent. "I'll never hit you, Asia, but it don't mean that you can put your hands on me without conse-quences."

"Well I'm fucking mad," she yells. She stands up and slides into her pink panties. The color next to her brown skin is picture perfect. "I did all of this work, and the only reason you think I'm doing it, is so you won't fuck some bucket head bitches around the way? Is that what you saying to me? Dane, that's fucked up, you don't care about me." She slides into her jeans, and bra.

"Asia, I'm a nigga. I don't give a fuck what you like, you didn't run anything past me. You just went out an applied for a scholarship you didn't even know that I wanted." I lit back up the bar. "That's sneaky and underhanded."

"I did it behind your back because I knew you wouldn't want to leave, home. I knew you would think about your brother, and your mother, instead of yourself. This is about your future, Dane. Don't you see?"

"You're right about one thing, this is *my* future, which is why you should've discussed it with me first. Asia, if we ever gonna make it, you can't be making moves like I'm some fucking kid. I keep telling you that shit, but you not listening." I inhale my weed, and it rushes through my lungs. "I'm seriously reconsidering this relationship."

She zips up her jeans and rushes over toward me. "Don't talk like that, Dane. I'm sorry. I just...I mean...don't you want a chance out of life? Don't you want to get away from DC too? You said it yourself that I would be a fool not to take this opportunity and the same thing should apply to you now."

"I'll leave when I get ready, Asia, but it's gonna be on my time."

"Dane, if you go to college you can make a life for yourself and your brother. I'm talking about life changes that will set you up forever. Don't you want it? Don't you deserve it?"

"I can't leave my family until—"

Loud banging at the door interrupts my statement.

"Dane, come out here, ma stabbing herself in the leg again," Tex yells. "I need you to help me hold her down!"

CHAPTER 6

TEX

"Ma, you can't swing the knife like that, you gonna stab yourself or somebody else!" When the knife hangs lower in her hand, I rush her, knocking her to the floor, like she a nigga on a football field. Asia grabs the knife and I try to pin her down but she's wiggling. "What the fuck is wrong with you?"

Her pink housecoat flies up, and exposes her white cotton panties. I feel like I'm gonna throw up. I finally get a hold of her.

"Get your god damn hands off of me, boy, I'm your mama." I'm pinning her down on the living room floor, next to the TV. "You better hold me down for as long as you can, mothafucka, because when I'm free, I'm coming for you. Do you hear what I'm saying? I'm coming for you, nigger! I'm talking murder!"

One minute she was looking at some old show called *Laverne & Shirley* on the tube, and the next minute she was cursing and talking about Pepsi don't go with milk. I don't even know what the fuck she talking about. I was outside paying the mobile window people who replaced our car window. When I came back inside to sit on the sofa with Logan and Ray, all of a sudden she started playing crazy and fucked up my high.

Moms suffers from schizophrenia, and if she don't take her meds, which is all of the time, she's a different person like now.

Dane walks over to me and takes the knife out of Asia's hand. "Ray-Ray, go into my mother's room and bring me that red pill bottle on her dresser."

"I don't want nobody in my fucking room, I done told ya'll niggers that shit before! Somebody is stealing my panties!"

He shakes his head. "Go head, Ray," I tell her. "It's cool. She ain't getting up."

She looks down at me still struggling with my mother. "But she told me the next time I went into her room, that she was gonna snatch my features off my face. I'm not trying to go back there, Dane."

"Bitch, go in there and get the fucking bottle," I say to her. "You go in there any other time when you sharing a blunt with her. What's the difference now?"

Dane hands Asia the knife. "Take it in the kitchen, babes." When she walks away he holds down my mother's legs. "Go ahead, Ray. I ain't letting her go."

Finally she walks into the back of the house. I got my mother's upper body, and Dane is holding down her legs. We look at each other and I'm sure he's probably thinking the same thing—we tired of going through shit like this. All our life our mother has been unstable. If she's not changing her mood at the drop of a dime, she's leaving the house for days on end, making us worry that someone killed or raped her. Or worse, that she just left and was never coming back again. I know Dane wants out of here just as much as I do, and one day we gonna do it together.

"I brought two bottles because I ain't know which one you wanted," Ray-Ray says to me. She holds up an orange and a red pill bottle.

"If one bottle is orange and the other bottle is red, which one do you think I want?" I ask her. "If I asked you for red?"

She shrugs. "Don't know, that's why I brought them both."

Ray-Ray got a pretty face but she's as dumb as a class full of F students. That's why I can never take her seriously, even though she wants me to be official with her. She doesn't have enough smarts to make me fall in love past the nut I bust inside of her. But she did give me the coolest son a nigga could ask for, and I give her credit for that if nothing else.

After we force three pills down mama's throat, we sit her up on the plush green sofa and wait for her to come down. Before long she isn't moving as much, and her eyes focus on us, her family, instead of everything else. The doctor said she only needed a pill a day, but he doesn't know our mother like we do. One of her red pills weren't even enough to make her nice enough to say hello in the morning.

When she's calm, Logan eases into her lap and rubs her thighs that are hanging out of her robe. Then he rests his head on her heart, and his wild curly hair brushes against her chin. "Love you, grandma."

"Love you too," she says, her tone resembling a zombie.

At least she responded.

"Ya'll might need to have her checked out again," Asia says. "She seems to be getting worse to me."

"Shut your bitch ass up. How the fuck you gonna come around here and make a comment 'bout a nigga's mother? You don't even know her like that. Stay in your fucking place."

"Tex, I love this one," Dane says to me. "I told you that before."

I look at Asia. Her expression is blank, but I know she's smiling inside. It probably does her good to know that my brother puts her before me.

That's how I know she's not the one, whether Dane knows it or not.

"I wasn't trying to interfere, Tex, I only want to help."

"Don't worry 'bout it, baby, Tex knows you didn't mean nothing by it." Dane kisses her on the cheek, but she's still looking at me. "Anyway, I gotta rap to you in private, Tex," Dane interrupts. "Come ride with me to the playground right quick." He kisses Asia again, as if the first time wasn't good enough. "You stay right here, I'll be back, baby."

"Aight, let me get the bars I rolled up earlier so we can fire up." I look at Ray. "Keep an eye on ma. If she starts tripping again, let me know."

She takes Logan off of her lap. "Okay, but hurry back, you know I hate to be alone with her when she's like this."

We hop in the car and drive to the playground where we go to hang out, and talk shit out. Dane sits on the bottom of the sliding board, and I lean against the ladder. The fire has already been lit on the blunt, so I pull and pass it to him.

"I can't believe after all this time, Ma still be wilding out. What the fuck? I hate not knowing what mood she gonna be in and when."

"You know she getting old," Dane says to me. "So now we gotta deal with her Skitz and her natural old age shit at the same time. We gonna be good though."

54

I laugh. "Man, I had a dream the other night right..."

"Oh shit, here you go with one of your wild ass dreams."

"This one was different." I take the bar from him. "It wasn't about me and you being in no field of weeds and fucking no random bitches either. I had a dream we was in this big house. It was all white with real green grass...like so green it looked fake. We were outside right, in the yard, riding our bikes. Red kids' bikes. But we was big, like how we are now. Anyway, I go inside the house, and I was talking to mama, and Uncle Larry."

Uncle Larry will forever be a sore topic with me. Even though he was our biological father, when I got older and learned he slept with my mother behind Marvin's back, I hated him for fucking up our family. I blamed him for being our father when Marvin was supposed to. The weird part is, if he didn't fuck my mother and get her pregnant, we wouldn't even be born. I'm confused.

"What was mama talking about?" Dane asks me.

"I think she was on her skitz shit again. I couldn't understand her. Anyway, I woke up after that because Ray-Ray put her ass on me and I wanted to fuck."

Dane laughs at me. "Nigga, you and Ray-Ray together is some dangerous and wild shit. The kick-er is that I can't see you being with nobody else on the long term. As much as ya'll fight, ya'll are going to be together forever."

I look at my brother. "Fuck you talking 'bout," I laugh. "Ain't nobody being together forever with no Ray-Ray. Me and you gonna get us a better crib like we talked about when we was kids. Now if she wanna still come over there and give me some of that pussy, I'm with that too. I swear I think the only reason I fuck with her is 'cause she got my son."

"I'm going to Te…"

Dane said something but I didn't hear him because I was getting more and more high. "What you say, nigga?"

"I said I'm going to Texas, to go to college. That's what I wanted to talk to you about."

I look over at him and laugh. "Yeah right. You don't give a fuck about no school. The only reason you be in class is to prove to them teachers that you smarter than them, and to fish for new bitches."

"I'm serious…I applied at Prairie View A & M University and I got in. Gotta full ride, little bro. I'm talking about books, school, living arrangements, and everything. They betting on the nigga and I'ma prove 'em right."

I look at him, and drop the half smoked blunt into the sand. He's serious and I focus on his eyes. I want to see if this is the same nigga who told me he would never leave my side, especially after all we went through. Who said we would always take care of each other because that's what brothers do.

"It was Asia wasn't it? I saw her going to the mailbox the other day. When I asked her what she was checking for, she said you leave her notes there when you not home. She did it didn't she? She applied for you to go to college and now like a sucker you going."

He doesn't respond. Just turns his head away.

"Don't you see what she's trying to do, Dane? Bitches like that don't like us to be together. They not use to the type of bond we got. Don't let her do this to us, man. We the Blake Brothers, this ain't what family does."

"I need this opportunity, Tex. It's not just for me, it's for you too. If I get a degree, I'll be able to get that house we talked about, and everything else! Shit, we could probably start our own boarding business since I know how much you love dogs." He smiles. "All that shit goes out of the window though if I don't take this ride."

"You sound just like that bitch of yours back there."

"Tex, you my brother, man, but I told you I love her. Please don't keep calling her out of her name, just 'cause you mad."

I'm so angry now that when I try to talk, my lips don't move. Fuck this nigga! If he wants to let her come between us, then that's on him, not me.

Blood is thicker than cum but I guess he didn't get the memo.

"You know what, I'm out here in the world on my own. And if something happens to me, then remember this day right here"— I point at the ground— "because it will be all your fault." I get into the car, and leave him at the playground without a ride.

CHAPTER 7

DANE

When Tex left me at the playground, I had
Asia come scoop me up in, *The Tin Man*, an old
Ford Escort Wagon that I only used when I ain't
have a choice. I bought it from a pipehead up the
block for a hundred dollars when he was trying to
get a rock. It cut off for no reason, smelled like an
old man, and was the ugliest thing I ever saw in my
life—but it was also all mine.

Me and Asia are riding around trying to find
Tex, so that I can talk some sense into him. We been
up and down the streets of DC, and every time I
pass a nigga who looks like him, I get annoyed.
Why he gotta act fucked up just 'cause I wanna better life for myself? And then there's the part of me
that knows what we went through in that house,
when Marvin left. I feel guilty. I'm starting to think
that going to college now, is not the right time.

59

"I can't believe your brother is doing this," Asia says looking out of her window. "This is so juvenile. He knew he was going to upset you if he left like that, and that's exactly what he did. Didn't he? He made you mad right?"

Here she goes with the dumb shit.

"You know how Tex is. He wear his feelings on his sleeve but he'll come around." I pull up on some dude who is wearing a similar blue shirt. Once again it's not him. "Tex will come 'round."

She looks at me. "So it really doesn't matter that he does this kind of shit all of the time?"

"What you getting at?"

"Are you having second thoughts about leaving for college? Because if you are, you need to re-think this whole thing." She brushes her long hair out of her face with her fingers. "Tex has been pulling this shit since the first day I got with you. Whenever he can't get his way, he tries to make you feel guilty. Sooner or later you're going to have to cut ties with him, baby. Maybe now is the time. And when you come back from school, hopefully by then he will have come to his senses."

My jaw tightens. "Do I tell you to cut your aunt off, even though she steals out of your purse every payday, because she can't stop the kleptomaniac voices from talking in her head?"

"Dane, that's—"

"Do I tell you to stop visiting your cousin, JB, even though it's obvious that he wants to fuck you? Did I tell you to drop your best friend, even though the bitch always got something to say about our relationship, even though she's sharing her nigga with her own mother?" She doesn't answer. "Do I, Asia?"

"No." her head drops.

"And you know why I don't do that?" I look over at her as I continue to drive the car. "I don't do it because that's your life and this is mine. So if I can respect you, why the fuck can't you respect me?"

"Because I'm scared for you, Dane."

"Scared of what?" I shrug. "I'm a grown as man."

"I'm scared you're not going to go."

I look out ahead of me. I remember the dream my brother had about us getting a new house, and living a better life. If I left Tex right now, he would do this type of sporadic shit all of the time, except I wouldn't be around to help him. "I can't do this to him right now, Asia. He needs me."

"What does he have over you?"

"It ain't about that." I pull the car over and park. "When that nigga who called himself our father left, it was me who took care of Tex. And he's not ready to let me go."

"You're gonna give up everything. For a grown ass man?"

I'm done arguing with her. "Aye, Asia, what's the rule on me waiting until later to go to college? Would the scholarship still be available, if I went next year or something?" I pull off to look for Tex again.

She looks at me with evil eyes. "You're serious aren't you?"

"I'm asking ain't I?"

"Stop the car, Dane."

I don't. Asia does this shit all of the time. We'll get into an argument, and when she can't get her way, she threatens to jump out while I'm driving. I'm trying to find my brother, and I don't have time for this shit right now either, so I keep it moving. She always talking about Tex giving me shit, but she the same way.

"Dane, I'm not fucking around. Either stop or I'm jumping out."

"If I pull this car over I'm not kissing your ass this time. I'm not gonna be driving behind you, while you fast walk up the street. I'm done with that shit."

"Nigga, you don't have to do shit but leave me the fuck alone," she yells, hitting me in the arm. "I ain't asking you to kiss my ass."

This bitch gonna make me kill her! Whenever she gets mad, she places her hands on me, and I'm sick of this shit. Now if I crack her jaw, I'd be wrong. But instead of laying hands on her, and being as ignorant as she is, I pull over in front of a liquor store.

Instead of getting out she looks at me. "Dane, you need to make a decision right here and right now." She points down. "Either you gonna pick me and go to college, or it's over between us tonight." She points at me. "I'm not gonna spend the rest of my life trying to compete with your brother anymore. I'm done with them games. So what's it gonna be?"

I look over at her. I don't say anything at first, because I want to stare at her pretty face. And then I say, "Get out, bitch, it's over."

The tears that fill up in her eyes are immediate. Before long they're rolling down her face. "You really want me to walk out of your life forever? Because if I do, I'm not coming back, Dane."

I turn toward my window. I can't look at her face anymore. "Bounce, Asia. I got more important things to do like find my brother. Blood is thicker than cum. Remember that shit."

When she gets out, I pull off before she can change her mind. I can hear her cries halfway up the block, but I don't stop. When I can't see her anymore, I remember the nigga who has been on the news lately, for raping girls in this neighborhood. My heart tugs and I'm tempted to go back and look for her. But, Asia gotta stop with the ultimatums. She can't come in the way of my brother, no matter what. And if I go back she always will.

I'm driving for an hour, and I still don't see Tex. I figure he'll come home when he's ready. Since I don't feel like going home, because I'm not trying to be around Ray-Ray who's always at our house, or my mother, I call Memory, a girl I met at the shoe repair store, when I was getting my Timbs cleaned awhile back in Baltimore. It wasn't long before I had her right where I wanted her. She got fired for cleaning my shoes for free, and ended up starting her side business, selling socks at the Baltimore flea market.

I take my phone out of my pocket and dial her number. When I hear her voice I say, "Memory..."

"Hey, sexy, I'm fucking you tonight?" she asks.

I smile. I got a fetish for women who say what's on their minds, and she is famous for it. "That's what I'm calling you for. What you over there doing?"

"Nothing that can't be stopped for you."

"You talk a lot of shit."

"It's true, plus I got a few steaks in the oven, some homemade mash potatoes on the stove, and I can throw some buttermilk biscuits in the oven if you really hungry."

"And why you gonna do all of that for me? At this time of night?"

"Because I'm extra horny, and you gonna need your energy."

I laugh, and turn my car around so I can catch the beltway. "I guess I'll be in B-more in forty minutes then."

"See you then sexy," she hangs up.

I take the Baltimore-Washington Pkwy to get to her house, smoking a blunt the entire way. Everything that happened today plays out in my mind. I'm missing Asia already, even though I know it will never work between us. With her going to Texas, she'll probably meet some lawyer type nigga, who's just as smart as she is, and be done with me all together. I guess it's for the best that we split up like this. We two different people.

When I make it to West Baltimore, to Memory's house, I'm thrown off. I blink a few times to be sure I'm seeing things straight. When I open my eyes again I know my mind isn't playing tricks on me. Asia is sitting on the steps of Memory's brownstone. My heart drops in my boxers because I didn't know she knew anything about Memory, let alone where she lived.

I park the bucket and get out to approach. "What you doing here?"

I can tell she has still been crying. "I thought about what you said about not going to college and all. So I made a decision too, Dane. And my decision goes like this, I can't live without you." She stands up and walks closer to me.

"Asia, what are you—"

"Shhhh"— she places her finger over my lips— "if getting an education means not having you in my life, it's not the kind of life I want." Suddenly she frowns. "But I'm not gonna give up my opportunity because I'm dumb enough not to see what a college degree can do for my future. No" — she shakes her head— "I'm going to give up my chance because I put so many bullet holes in that bitch upstairs, that it will be like she never existed." She raises her shirt and shows me her gun, before letting her shirt drop down. "Because if I can't have you, neither will she."

"Asia, what the fuck are you doing?" I try to whisper since we are outside and she's tripping. I look up the block to see who's watching. Thankfully nobody.

"You know exactly what I'm doing, nigga. You brought me to this point." She turns around to walk up the stairs, but I pull her back and hold her.

"Don't do that," I hug her tightly. I can feel the handle of the gun pushing into my thigh because she's so much shorter than me. "You too smart for this kind of shit."

"Get off me, Dane." She tries to wiggle out of my arms but I don't let her. "I'm serious. If you giving up your future, I'm giving up mine too, by way of first degree murder."

"I'll go, baby."

"Get off of me," she says, as she continues to move.

"Did you hear me?" I squeeze her arms and look down at her. "I said I'll go." She looks up at me. "You wild as shit for this move, Asia. How the fuck you even knew where I was going?"

"Because I let you have her, Dane. I figured if I didn't shut this situation down, like I did the rest, that I'd be able to find you when I needed you. So I need you now and I'm here. But if you think I'm gonna let that bitch take you from me, you got another thing coming."

I kiss her lips, grab her ass and pull her toward me again. I can smell the lemon scent of her hair. I love this bitch, so much. "Asia, if we gonna do this thing again, you gotta let me handle my family. It ain't for you to manage that situation no more. It's on me. And stop putting your hands on me, I'm not a child and you not my mother."

"Okay, baby. Whatever you say."

When my phone vibrates in my pocket, and I read the text, my heart drops. "What is it, Dane? Is everything okay?"

"We gotta go, Tex was just stabbed!"

CHAPTER 8

TEX
(AN HOUR EARLIER)

I'm on top of Bird, with my dick shoved inside her pussy, while Ray-Ray is underneath us, licking my balls and licking her clit. I can feel my blood making my dick harder, while her pussy gets wetter. This shit is beyond hot, and I'm surprised Ray-Ray went along with the threesome especially after all of that shit she did earlier tonight with breaking my car window.

"Mmmmm," Bird moans, biting on her bottom lip, before she sucks her own nipples.

Bird is a sexy girl, about five feet, with big breasts, a little bit of stomach and a fatter ass. She's just my speed. Not too skinny and not too fat. I don't know what my real obsession with Bird is about. If I had to pin point a reason, I would say it's because she was the only bitch I went after but couldn't get. I love a challenge.

After I got into it with my brother, and told Ray-Ray I was stressed, she agreed to the three-some. Her only thing was that I don't look into Bird's eyes while I was inside of her, which is easier said than done. This bitch is super sexy!

"Damn, Tex"— Bird whispers— "this dick feeling right. Keep it right there, Daddy."

I lower my eyes and shake my head. The look I give her warns her against talking to me while we're fucking. I didn't want Ray-Ray to think that me and her would hook up again without her, even though it was on my mind.

Bird whispers, "But I can't help it."

"Fuck me from the back, while I lay on top of her so I can suck her titties," Ray-Ray says, as she rubs my shoulders from behind. "I feel like a wash rag down here licking around your dick and her ass. Who gonna hook me up? I wanna get fucked too."

FUCK! Ray-Ray is blowing me! I fuck her on a daily basis, so it ain't like we don't do our thing. I kinda wanted to stash inside Bird's wet walls a little longer, but if I said anything but okay to Ray, she would turn it into a whole different situation.

We make the quick transitions. Bird is still ly-ing face up while Ray-Ray crouches over her. Since Ray is on all fours, I push into her asshole instead. I had been brutal on her pussy over the years, sticking anything into her I could find, and now it can't hold a dick tight enough to make me bust. If I wanted to get mine off with Ray, I had to fuck her in her second pussy. Her asshole.

As I'm banging her from the back, I'm watching her pink tongue roll over Bird's nipple. Although Bird is moaning, she's looking directly into my eyes. It's as if we're the only ones here. Bird is so fucking sexy I can't wait for us to get together again, maybe without Ray-Ray if I can slide away from her long enough.

Ray must feel me giving Bird too much attention because all of a sudden, she squeezes the walls of her asshole tightly. I don't know where she learned that shit, but it immediately makes me refocus on her, and I'm reminded about how good we fuck together. *Sorry, Bird, but you fucking with a pro now.* I grab a hold of Ray's waist, and pound into her deeper and harder.

I'm just about to spray my nut into her body when she does a thumping sensation through her inner walls, which feels like she's stroking the nut out of me.

"Work that shit, bitch!"

When I'm empty I fall into Ray's back, which forces her flat on top of Bird's body. My sweat rolls down the sides of Ray's waist, and rolls on top of Bird's stomach. We untangle ourselves and I lie in the middle of them. Bird on my left and Ray-Ray on my right.

Rubbing my stomach I say, "Bird, what you got in there to eat? A nigga famished."

"Everything, I keep a stocked fridge at all times."

I smile. "Cool, you should go out there and make me a sandwich. I eat anything, plus after all that, I'm hungry like shit."

She hops up and I get a chance to look at her body again. A small line of hair runs down her pussy and my dick jumps. When I look to my left Ray is in my face, frowning. She don't miss a thing. Old Hawk Eyes.

"You want me to make you a grilled cheese sandwich with garlic potatoes?" She slides into her red panties and bra. "I got some cold beer in there too. I must warn you, I'm known around the world for my food. You gonna be hooked."

"Bird, you should chill, I'll go cook for him." Ray-Ray jumps up. "I don't want nobody cooking for my man but me, no offense. Even though I let you sample the dick." She slides into her sweat pants, no shirt and dips out of the room. "Don't be back here fucking...I'm a murderer," she yells from the hallway.

I pull Bird towards me and slob her down. Then I sit on the edge of the bed, and grab her so that she's sitting on my lap. I slide her panties to the side and push her on my hard dick. I fuck her while I keep my eyes on the door. Knowing that Ray-Ray can come back into the room at anytime and kill us, makes me harder. Bird is biting down on her bottom lip and I'm digging into her pussy so hard that it doesn't take me long to cum into her. I kiss her again and she stands up.

I wipe my dick with her shirt on the floor, and she fixes her panties. We try to act like we didn't fuck again.

"Why you tell Ray-Ray I called you? If you were gonna give me the pussy anyway? Don't you think that was a waste of time?"

She shrugs. "I don't know...I guess I was mad." She crawls to the top of the bed and leans up against her headboard.

"What would you be mad about? You got me confused like shit, shawty."

"I don't know...I mean...she keeps saying how much you love her, and how you would never look at another girl. I guess it made me jealous to think that you were all serious about her, when you faked like you wanted to be with me too."

"Look, I don't know about all that other shit you talking about, but it's like this. I want to fuck you again, and I want to keep it between us. Is that something you can deal with or not?"

"Not," she says, "I rather keep this shit right here."

"Why you playing hard to get?"

She shrugs. "I got my reasons, and it don't have nothing to do with you."

Ray-Ray comes back a few minutes later with food for all three of us. At first I'm trying to figure out what's up with Bird. When I realize it probably doesn't matter anyway, I drop it. It's evident that she wants me.

We're eating and for some reason, while I got two naked bitches around me, I think of my brother again. I hate that he's letting Asia come between us. She ain't nothing but some square bitch trying to break us up and split us apart.

"What you thinking about," Ray-Ray asks me while drinking her beer. "You look mad about something."

"It ain't nothing I'm gonna tell you about."

"You thinking about Asia again right?"

"I just don't know why he want to go to college." I say. "It ain't like he ever thought about it before. Now all of a sudden he gotta scholarship, the shit is just dumb."

"Maybe he's trying to become something better," Ray says. "Don't you want something better for me and Logan? If you ask me I admire Dane for going away from some place that he's known all of his life. DC is starting to get whack."

I don't give a fuck about wanting something better for you, bitch. But my son gonna be straight.

"That's not what I'm saying, Ray. And since you don't know nothing real about the matter, don't speak on it."

It's quiet for a while until Bird says, "Did you tell him about my neighbor upstairs. And how he made you cry?"

I look at Ray-Ray. "What happen?"

"It was dumb," she says waving me off.

"Don't tell me it's dumb." I grab her upper arm. "What the fuck happen?"

"He said my ass was lopsided when I was coming to visit Bird earlier tonight. I don't even know why she told you that. It ain't like—"

I'm already on my feet and out the door. I can hear them running behind me, but it doesn't make me move any slower. "Which door?" I ask one of them.

"5D," Bird says. "Upstairs. But what you gonna do?"

I'm at his door in five seconds and bang real hard. I don't know his name or who I'm even looking for. When a nigga wearing blue boxers, no shirt opens the door, I steal him smack in the jaw.

I didn't see the kitchen knife he had in his hand before I moved on him, but I felt it later.

CHAPTER 9

DANE

I'm yelling at the officer at the front desk. I don't understand if my brother was stabbed, why he's in jail. "Sir, you have to tell me what's going on. I was told my brother was stabbed and I don't understand why he isn't in a hospital. No disrespect but you seem real nonchalant about this shit, that's why I'm so mad."

The officer looks at a stack of papers, pasted to a brown clipboard in front of him. "And like I told you before, when I find out what is going on I'll let you know. You can't make me tell you nothing I don't know. But if you keep pressing the matter, you won't have to wonder if he's back there because you'll be able to see for yourself. Now have a fucking seat, before I lose what's left of my patience with you."

"Nig—" I'm about to go at him until Asia pulls my arm.

75

"Don't do this, Dane. Let's just sit down and wait to see what he has to say. "Please, baby. Not like this."

I look at the officer and decide to calm down. If I'm locked up I can't help my brother and I won't be good to anybody. My heart feels like it's about to jump out my chest, because I always know what's going on with my brother.

I still don't understand what's happening. One minute I'm in Baltimore trying to convince Asia not to stab my sidepiece, and the next thing I know Ray-Ray is texting me that my brother was stabbed.

I sit in one of the hard plastic black seats, across from the officer. I'm staring him down, not all the way sure I won't punch this mothafucka in the face. "He's fine," Asia says softly, placing her hand over mine. "Try not to worry about him. He's a big boy, Dane. Trust me things will work out."

"You don't understand. He told me if anything happened to him it would be my fault. And now he gets stabbed? How can I not carry this shit on my heart?"

She shakes her head slowly. "What happened tonight isn't your fault, baby. Tex got caught up in some shit, and got hurt...that's it, and that's all. Look at the good part, if he's here he can't be hurt badly." She sighs. "Baby, I want you to remain positive, because you have a tendency to fly off of the handle and make things worse than they are."

I look into her eyes. "Remain positive as in still go to college? Because if that's what you're talking about, Asia, we ain't talking."

"I just don't want this incident to push you all the way back, Dane. That's all I'm saying. Tex is a grown man, with a son and family of his own. You have to let him do him. We not getting any younger, we're getting older, and the opportunity you received with the scholarship doesn't come all of the time. Plus if you don't go to college, all that shit you said to me earlier would be a lie. And I hate to be lied to. Just like you hate to be bossed around."

I clench my fists. "Asia, shut the fuck up with all this dumb shit! The only thing I'm thinking about right now is Tex. That's it, and that's all."

She throws her hands up in the air and leans back into the seat. It squeaks a little. "All I can do is be real with you, Dane." She says under her breath. "If you want a bitch to tell you what you want to hear so that it will sound good, maybe I should've let you fuck Memory. Sometimes I think I'm too much woman for you."

I shake my head and laugh. "You always find a way to bring up the past. Always. Why is that?"

"I'd think you'd appreciate living in the past, since that's all you keep talking about. In my opinion you don't care about anything that has to do with the future."

I'm about to walk outside and wait on news from my brother, to get away from her annoying ass, when I see Tex strut out of the back of the precinct. His lower arm is bandaged, close to his wrist, and he has blood all over his jeans.

I stand up and he walks toward me. I rush up to him and grip him into a hug. I push him back and observe his bandage. "What the fuck happen, Tex? Who did this shit? Give me the address and I can be on my way now."

"It's not worth it, anyway it's dumb," he says under his breath. "I'm sorry to even put you through all this shit, man. It's a complete waste of time and Ray shouldn't have called you. I told her to get the money to bail me out but she was broke."

"Why you get stabbed? Is it somebody I know?"

"It doesn't matter why I was stabbed. And thanks for bailing me out." He looks down at the grungy floor. "But can we talk?" He looks over my shoulder. "Brother to brother?"

I look back at Asia. "Yeah...let me go rap to her right quick. We drove here together but I'll find a way to get her home."

He frowns at her and says, "I'll be waiting for you outside." I throw him the keys to the Tin Man. "Try not to be too long."

I walk over to Asia, and hold her hands into mine. Before I can say anything she says, "Don't tell me, you want me to catch a cab home."

"Where did all that come from?" I say, mad she knew before I could say anything.

"Cut the shit, Dane. Just keep it real."

"I can put you in a cab or you can take the car and we'll catch a cab." I shrug. "I just have to talk to Tex in private, and we can't do it with you in the car. He seems like he wants to tell me something important, and after everything that went down tonight, I figure I'll give him that time."

"You mean he doesn't want to tell you anything in front of me, because he doesn't like me." She rolls her eyes. "It's cool though. I'll catch the cab, but you need to tell your brother that I'm not going anywhere. And one of these days we're going to have to learn to get along, especially since I have plans to be your wife." She kisses me softly on the cheek. "And after you tell him that, tell him that I was worried, and I'm glad he is okay."

She walks away from me and pushes out the front door. I follow her out and surprisingly a cab pulls up directly in front of us. She waves, enters the cab and drives off. I walk up to my bucket and slide inside. Tex is already inside waiting, with a bar lit up, right in front of the police department.

"She threw the fuck you sign up in the air at me," Tex says. "I don't care what we do I doubt very

seriously we will ever get along. I'm not even gonna
try anymore."

"I hope you don't mean that, man."

"Look…I don't wanna talk about her tonight."
He sighs. "While I was in the cell I had a lot of time
on my hands to think."

"You act like you did fifteen upstate," I laugh.

"I'm serious, nigga." He tosses the rest of the
blunt out of the window. "Even an hour is too much
time to be in that mothafucka. Anyway, I thought
about this college thing and I really want that for
you."

"Holdup," I smile, "what the fuck they do to
you in there? Not even five hours ago you were giving me the blues."

He shakes his head and laughs. "I'm not gonna
lie, I did get a little mad at first. But I can't stop you
from doing what you wanna do either. I just hope
it's a choice you wanna make and not one that your
girlfriend is making for you. That's all I'm saying."

"When have you ever known me to take orders
from anybody? All my choices are my own."

"I don't know, man, you just seem different
now that's all."

"Well regardless of what you think I'm still the
same, and even when I leave for college I'm going
to be the same." I open up the glove compartment,
and pull out two freshly rolled bars. I hand him one
and I keep the other. After lighting mine, I light his.

"So you gonna tell me now what happened?" When my phone goes off I quickly answer it.

"Dane, is Tex with you? Logan just choked, and he almost died. I'm at your house. He gotta come now!"

I swear Ray-Ray is always the bearer of bad news.

CHAPTER 10
TEX

Today is turning out to be the worst day of my life. As I push open the doors to my house I have one thing on my mind. Please let my son be okay.

Once I'm inside I look at Logan who is sitting on the couch wearing only his diaper. A big chunk of hot dog is sitting on the floor a few feet in front of him. I already know what happened.

"Ray, please tell me you didn't let him swallow chunks of hot dogs again after I begged you not to," I say. "Please tell me you not that stupid, and that you almost didn't kill our child."

The door closes behind me and I realize it's my brother.

"He had to eat, Tex! I mean what do you want me to do starve him to death? You know this boy eats me out of house and home around here."

"Bitch, you in my house!"

82

"You know what I mean." She pauses. "Plus I only stepped into the kitchen a quick second to get a beer, and he was holding his throat."

"You, stupid bitch! You can't do the most basic of things. It ain't about him eating, I'm not even talking about that. Please don't tell me you're that dumb enough to believe that I don't want you to feed him. This is about you being irresponsible and treating him like he's a man instead of a fucking child."

"You act like I'm the one who tried to give him weed earlier, don't talk to me about being irresponsible. You don't get the Daddy Dearest Award neither."

"Did you take him to the doctors?" Dane asks. He lifts Logan up, and my son wraps his arms around his neck. "He could have problems later if you don't get him tested."

"No," she responds rotating her neck. "I didn't take him yet."

"Yo, Ray, why didn't you take him to the doctors? I would've thought that would be the first thing you'd do. You not even making sense right now."

"I couldn't find my Medicaid card. And I wasn't about to go to no doctor and have them ring up a bunch of charges under my name. All for them to tell me that he choked on a hot dog and is fine."

I'm on my way to lay hands on her, and thinking about how hard I'm going to choke her, when my brother sits Logan down and pushes me back. "You not about to hit her in front of your son who almost died." He pauses. "Look, walk with me to the playground, and let's talk it out." I'm still breathing heavily. "Tex, walk with me, man. Shit gonna be cool."

I turn around and face Ray-Ray. "You better be looking for my son's card while I'm gone too. If it's not here when I get back, for the first time since we've fucked with each other, I'm gonna hit you so hard you gonna be knocked out for weeks."

We end up at the park. I'm sitting on the sliding board and he's standing next to me. We're passing a bar back and forth since we don't have much of the pack from Wico left. We smoke that much on a regular basis.

"If you gonna go to college, I been thinking about something," I tell him. "I was gonna say it to you before Ray called about Logan."

"Aw shit, whenever you think about anything, I feel like trouble is coming."

I laugh. "No serious, you see how shit is at home, man. I'm not gonna be able to handle all of the bills and responsibility by myself. I got ma, an irresponsible baby mother and my kid to look after."

He inhales the blunt and hands it to me. "Get to the point, man."

"If you gonna go to college, let's do one last hit before you go. But if we do it, we have to make it a big one."

"I'm listening."

"One that's gonna pay off. Maybe we can hit Mrs. Swanson's fat ass. Anybody spending fifteen thousand dollars for a Cavalier King Charles Spaniel, got money enough to pass around. Plus did you peep the diamonds around that bitch's neck from when she dropped off her dog last month?"

"Naw...I'm not fucking with her. She good peoples and ain't never did us wrong."

"You right," I nod. "What about Mr. Brinson...the dude who drops off his German Shepard every other Saturday? He's an asshole, plus he got paper. Remember that time he dropped his dog off and claimed we didn't wash him, or feed him in a week? And the boss wrote us up for neglect? When you know how serious I be 'bout dogs?"

"I know, man, but you threatened the nigga too. If he does get robbed, who you think they gonna look at first?"— he points at me— "you."

My brother thinks too hard about the jobs we be casing sometimes. I think he did the past jobs with me just because I asked him too, and he was worried something would happen to me.

"Just let me handle finding the perp," I say to him. "I got things under control."

"I'm not fucking around with you, Tex. We not doing nobody you beefed with at the shop, and that includes the two mothafuckas you just named."

"Trust me."

"I'm serious."

"Just trust me, Dane. I ain't gonna do nothing to jeopardize me or you. You'll see."

CHAPTER 11

DANE

I'm at the counter, at my job, giving a teacup yorkie it's heartworm medicine. While Tex has been walking around like shit is cool, like he doesn't have a problem in the world, my mind is wrecked.

Since I've worked here, we robbed at least fifteen houses. It could be more, but some of them were a waste of time because they never had any money. But today feels different. My stomach is churning because I have a bad feeling about going through with our plan tonight. Something tells me that the job we got planned, is gonna backfire in our face, and I'm not sure how.

When I'm done giving the puppy its meds, I hand him back over to the owner, so she can say goodbye before she leaves. "He should be good with what I gave him for about three months."

"Thank you, Dane," Mrs. Parnell says to me, rubbing her dog's head. "I really appreciate you taking care of Pops for me. I wouldn't be able to enjoy my trip because I would be worrying about him so much."

While I'm talking to her, Tex comes from the backroom, takes the dog out of her arms and kisses him in the mouth. Their tongues press against each other and I think I'm about to lose my food. I think his dick gets hard when he be doing that shit or something.

"You don't worry about nothing, Mrs. Parnell," He says. "Pops gonna be good here. You already know how I am when it comes to the dogs. Just take your vacation and relax your mind."

She grins like a proud mother. "I have to be honest, Tex, Pops has been to lots of boarding facilities and this is by far the cleanest and best. Whenever he comes here, he's always happier than he was when I dropped him off. It does my heart proud."

"I don't do nothing but give him love." He rubs the dog's head, a little too roughly if you ask me. "Don't worry. So, Mrs. Parnell, where you off too for vacation this time? Didn't you just come back from the Bahamas?"

"I try to travel at least a few times a year, it helps me relax."

"Wow, you must have a real wealthy lifestyle to be able to afford so many vacations. You want an adopted son?"

Although Mrs. Parnell giggles, I feel like stealing this nigga in his right jaw. Even if we wanted to hit her house, after the scene that he's making, she would be sure to point the cops our way.

"You are such a wonderful young man, and if I ever do think about adopting, I'll consider you." She blushes.

"So is your husband going with you?"

"What difference does it make," a black man dressed in a navy blue suit asks, walking up behind her. He flashes a gold badge at us. "She's dropping off the dog, not telling you her life story." He stuffs the badge back into his pocket. "If you ask me you're getting a little too personal."

I feel as if my life flashed before my eyes. I knew this morning would turn out to be terrible, and that's exactly what's happening. I'm not going to college, a nigga is going to jail. I'm gonna get a full ride there too.

Mrs. Parnell looks at the officer and says, "Well, let me go, boys." She observes the officer again with anger in her eyes. I guess she wasn't feeling how he came at us. "I have a plane to catch and don't want to miss it." She rubs her puppy again. "I'll see you boys and my dog in about a week."

When she leaves I look at the officer. "Can I help you with something, sir?" I look down at the counter, and try to arrange a box of heartworm medicines that didn't need arranging.

"Where is the owner?" he asks me. "Of this boarding facility? I've called several times but can never seem to catch him."

I look over at my brother who is staring at the officer so harshly, I'm afraid he's going to get in trouble for the look alone. "What is this about?" I ask him.

He leans in. "Are you the owner?"

"I'm in charge of the store, while he's gone," I say. "Anyway the owner is never here."

"What's your name?"

I clear my throat. "Dane...Dane Blake."

"And you?" He looks at Tex.

"He's my brother, Tex." I reply for him.

"Well, Dane, since you're in charge I'll hold you responsible for riddling me this question. There have been a string of robberies recently in this neighborhood, and do you know what they all have in common?" He picks up a doggy breath mint, opens it and drops it into his mouth.

Pops starts barking hysterically at the cop, and Tex rubs his head, I guess to calm him down. I don't think he fucks with his thieving ass.

"I don't know but I guess you gonna tell me."

He sucks on the mint. "They all have one thing in common, each one of them have left their animals at this place to be boarded. Why do you think that is?"

"We don't know why that is because it isn't any of our business," Tex says. "How 'bout you do your fucking job and tell us."

"Tex," I yell. "I got this." I put my hand out. "Relax, and go take Pops to his crate in the back."

"But I want to—"

"Go," I yell, pointing toward the back. "I said I got it."

He walks toward the door and says, "Aight, but I'm coming right back." He looks at the officer again and then leaves.

"Your brother sounds like he has an attitude. You might want to calm him down, maybe put one of them leashes around his neck, before he finds himself behind bars, with people like him." He takes another doggy mint and pops it into his mouth. "Because although I'm a sport, my colleagues might not be so nice."

"We don't know nothing about no robberies. Officer..."

"Stern. I'm officer Stern."

"Like I said, Officer Stern, we don't have any information for you, I'm sorry I couldn't be of more assistance. Now if you know something we don't, you just do what you gotta do. Other than that I gotta get back to work."

He reaches into his pocket, and throws five dollars on the counter, along with his business card. "It's for the mints. Keep the change. I'm sure I'll be seeing you again soon."

When he leaves I call Tex back out front, and lock the door, even though we don't close for hours. "We can't fuck with it, man! The burglaries are over! That cop is onto us. He knows we been setting niggas up. I knew it was just a matter of time before this came back to haunt us and that's exactly what it did."

"He don't know shit," he says bouncing his red ball off the counter. "If he did we would be locked up right now." He picks up his business card, looks at it and stuffs it into his pocket. "Trust me, he's just fucking with us to see if he can get into our head."

"You not even listening, Tex. The man said that this boarding facility is the common factor, of everybody who has been robbed. If he doesn't know it will be just a matter of time before he catches on to us. The shit is off."

"Well what about me? You making decisions without even thinking about where I'm gonna be when you go off to college."

"Are you listening to yourself?" I frown.

"No, are you listening to yourself?" he points at me. "If we don't do this job how the fuck am I gonna take care of the family? You abandoning us, man. And the shit ain't right."

"You act like you gonna get a million dollars from this gig!"

"It don't matter, Dane! Now just because some cop who doesn't have anything on us came sniffing around here, you getting all scared."

"You heard what I said right, Tex. The shit ain't up for discussion."

"I heard you, but what if I don't wanna listen? It ain't like I need you to do a job, I've done plenty of them by myself before."

"If you do that then you don't have shit else to say to me. I'm dead serious."

"You wanted it that way not me."

CHAPTER 12

DANE

I'm sitting in the passenger seat of our car, smoking a bar. I got a lot of shit on my mind. I wanna know what this cop has on us, and if he's holding out by not telling us everything he knows. I look behind us. Maybe he's following us for now. I don't see anybody though. And then there's this college shit. I'm not sure, but I don't know if this is for me or not. The last thing on my mind is Asia. I don't know where she is.

I had been calling that girl all day, with no luck of getting her on the phone. I didn't just hit her house phone and her cell, I also called her best friend and she claimed she hadn't seen her either. It ain't like her not to answer my calls. Any other time she'd be burning my cell phone minutes up and I'd have to put her off, because she'd be calling me and not talking 'bout shit.

"Still trying to call that bitch huh?" Tex asks me, as he steers the car down the street. "That chick really do got you fucked up. I swear, out of all of the bitches you came across in your time, I couldn't see her being the one to open your nose. If you ask me Memory, is badder than she is anyway. That's just my opinion though."

I shake my head. He's calling her multiple bitches to get me mad but I don't give in. Plus once again he not saying shit I wanna hear. "So you speaking to me now. Because you was acting like a bitch earlier."

"I never wasn't speaking to you. I just don't like you being soft all of a sudden. If you let one nigga come on the job and get you shook, maybe this life was never for you."

"If by soft you mean keeping us out of jail, I'm as soft as cotton. Don't forget you haven't been out of jail long, Tex. You got court coming up next month and everything. You sure you trying to add breaking and entering to your charges? I would think you'd be the first one who wanna back off."

"Yeah whatever."

My phone rings. When I see who's calling I shake my head. I started to let it ring, but if something is wrong I wouldn't be able to forgive myself. "Where you been, Asia?"

"What do you want?" she asks with an attitude.

"First off you calling me."

"That's because you've been ringing my phone like you're crazy, Dane, and unlike what you might believe, I have shit to do too. Like get ready for college."

I look at the phone. "Hold up, you playing me like that?"

"I'm just saying if you—"

I hung up on her. I don't feel like her shit right now either. If she wants to come at me like that then I guess we done. As long as I know she's safe, I'm good on everything else. When my phone rings again, I ignore it. It's not until she calls me five more times that I finally answer.

"What?" I put my right foot on the dashboard of the car, and look out the window.

"Why you keep hanging up," Asia says crying. "I...you...don't"—she sniffles— "I don't understand how you want me to feel. I want the best for you, Dane. I don't want you to have to worry about not getting what you want out of life. Plus DC too dangerous for you. Do you remember what happened the last time you and your brother got into a fist fight?"

"Asia, don't—"

"Do you," she screams.

I don't answer.

"The fight was so bad your back had to be stitched up because you fell on a glass beer bottle.

You didn't even want to go to the doctors until the shit started itching and oozing green gel"—she sniffles—"I can't be worried about you anymore, Dane, while I'm in college. I need to know what you want to do. Are you going with me or—"

"I'm going."

"Or what," she continues not listening to me. "The time is now to make a decision, Dane. I can't take this anymore. I won't take this anymore."

"Baby, stop fussing, I said I'm going."

"Stupid ass nigga, let a bitch guilt trip him into going to college," Tex says under his breath. I look over at him. "I'm not saying nothing else. You already know how I feel about the matter, I'm just letting you know again."

Focusing on Asia I say, "Like I said, I'm going to school, but it's not because you're trying to make me feel guilty. It's because I really want to see how far I can go, and before now I didn't see the possibilities. If shit work out right, maybe this will be better for me. Whatever the situation, I really want to follow through this time, so relax, I'm with you on this."

"I love you so much, Dane. You're gonna see, this is the best thing you can do for yourself. And for our relationship too."

The car stops, and we are in a neighborhood I'm not familiar with. My brother grabs something I can't see from under the seat, and stuffs it under his shirt. "I'll be right back," he says to me before getting out.

"Where are we?" I ask him.

"At a friend's house. Just chill, and talk to your chic, before she loses her mind. I'll be right back.

As he walks out I focus on Asia again. She's saying something but it's the tail end of what she says that I catch. "I love you too, Asia. You know I do."

"Then marry me," she says.

"Baby...I don't...."

"Please, Dane. Why we keep going through this fighting shit if we gonna be together anyway. I mean if you marry me I'll make you the happiest man on earth. I promise. You won't regret being with me not one day."

"Why do you keep asking me to marry you? Didn't I say when we get married, it will be because I asked you. Don't you want the fairy tale?"

"Fuck the fairy tale, I want you to say yes! And I don't need you to ask me to be your wife to make it happen, I just want to take care of you, Dane. Please let me."

The phone is still on my ear when I notice the name on the mailbox in front of the house, on the curb. It sends chills down my spine when I read the name. *Martin*. She's one of our biggest customers and I know this nigga is not crazy enough to rob her, especially with the officer snooping around the job.

"Asia, I gotta go, baby."

"What's wrong?"

"I just gotta go. I'll holla at you when I can."

I throw the phone in the seat, get out of the car and look around. When I don't see any nosey neighbors, I enter the Iron Gate surrounding the property and move toward the backyard. My heart is beating with every step I take. When I bend the side of the house my worst nightmare is realized. Tex is at the door holding an iron rod, trying to break in. But since I normally pop the locks, and disarm the security systems, he doesn't know what he's doing.

"I know you not this fucking stupid," I whisper.

"Go back to the car."

"Tex, what the fuck are you doing?" I jog up the stairs and hit him in the back of the head with a closed fist, and his face presses against the door. "I told you we weren't fucking with this job. And you deliberately disobey me?"

"Did you say disobey?" he asks. "You not my father!"

"Tex, I'm not doing this shit."

"Then go back to the phone and make love to your precious girlfriend. Because with or without you, I'm going inside."

I contemplate leaving him, because something tells me that going inside; will change the rest of my life. But he's my kid brother, and I can't let him do this shit by himself, no matter how much I want to.

I snatch the rod from him. "Move back, I got this."

"Put these on first." He hands me a set of latex gloves from his pocket and I slide them on. Within a second I'm inside of the house.

The house is plush, and it smells of vanilla and cleaning products. We're in the kitchen so I grab a trash bag and stuff everything of value inside it. Once I'm done, in there we move throughout the house to see what else we can get. I can't believe how much shit she has in this joint.

Already I eye about ten thousand dollars worth of electronics. I mean she has iPads lying around the dining and the living room, Wii systems and large TV's. I already know if we back the car up we'll make out clean just taking everything not bolted down. I toss the iPad and the Wii's into the bag. I'm in goon mode as I go through the house until I see my brother's fearful expression.

"What is it," I ask him dropping the bag. It makes a thud to the floor. "Why you looking all crazy? The cops coming or something?"

"Don't be mad, man."

I step up to him. "What the fuck is it?"

"She's home. She's in the tub."

"Who's home?"

"Mrs. Martin. What we gonna do now?"

CHAPTER 13

DANE

I'm sitting on the edge of the tub with Mrs. Gayle Martin's large naked body between my legs. My hand is pressed against her trembling lips, and I'm squeezing so tight I can feel her teeth push back. I need to keep her silent, so that whoever is knocking at the door, will go away. One minute he's saying Mrs. Martin is here, and the next someone is knocking.

This can't be the way. This can't be what we have to do to make a living. I know there's better, and I was almost there. In college, ready to have it all. Now all that is about to be over, because of a mistake.

Tex is at the closed door, with a gun, looking as if he's about to blast anyone who tries to come inside. I remember when he got that shit too, and I should've taken it from him then. He bought it off of this kid who bought it for protection, but was in a car accident before he had a chance to use it. Still, after all this time, I hoped he'd never have a reason to pull it out. The only relief I feel is that there aren't any bullets in it.

"I don't hear them knocking anymore, D," Tex says with his ear pressing against the wooden door. He looks back at me. "I think we good."

"Are you sure?"

"As sure as I'm going to be anyway."

I look down at the woman between my legs. Her large brown breasts hang over the sides of her body, and look like two bean bags. I don't wanna hurt her, but I needed time to think of a plan, before we let her go.

"Listen, I'm gonna take my hand off of your mouth, but if you scream I'm gonna be mad, and I don't know what I'm liable to do. Do you understand me?"

She nods yes.

My hand peels away from her wet lips. Mrs. Martin runs her tongue over her mouth and says, "I can't believe ya'll are doing this shit." She looks at me and then my brother. "Do you know who I am? Do you have any idea about what I can do to you?"

I look at Tex who avoids me by looking at the floor. This is all his fault and I'm trying not to hate him in the moment because it won't help our situation.

"Mrs. Martin, I know it's fucked up, but we aren't trying to hurt you," I say. "You always tip us good when you pick your dog up and we fuck with you like that."

"Not trying to hurt me?" she laughs. "It's too late for that. My son is going to go off once he hears about this."

"Well maybe we'll make sure he doesn't get the message then," Tex says walking up to her with the gun aimed toward her face. "Because if that's our only problem, we don't have a problem now do we?"

I slap the barrel down and it fires into the floor. I back up because I didn't know he had bullets. "Tex…is that…is that shit loaded?"

"You thought it was a game?"

"What is going on with you? Are you that far gone in your head that you don't realize what's happening? We in over our heads now, Tex."

I hear the water splashing around and look back at Mrs. Martin who is still in the tub. She's beyond mad, she has a look in her eye that could kill us, and I think we are in too deep immediately.

"Listen, boys, I like both of you." We look at her. She doesn't bother hiding her body. "Whenever I bring my precious Heidi to you, you take care of her. And I never had a problem with you fellas. So I'm gonna do it like this."

Mind you she still hasn't covered her breasts.

"You two niggas get out of my house right now, and leave town, and I won't tell my son Mercury about none of this. It will be as if nothing happened. But if you take this option, and proceed with my good graces, know that you better take everyone you love with you. Because if I see either one of you in these streets, or your family members, I'm ridding the world of you and everybody you love."

"And if we don't leave town," Tex yells.

"Then me and mines are burying niggas for the next six months in D.C. It's as simple as that."

Before I can stop Tex from reaching her, he comes down over her face with the butt of his gun. Her cheek opens up like a watermelon, and blood splashes out of her skin and drips into the tub. I grab him by the waist and tackle him to the wet bathroom floor. The gun drops out of his hand, and I crawl over to it, stuff it in the waist of my jeans and grab him by the shoulders.

"Get off of me, nigga," he says. He's trying to push me off but I don't budge. I always have been stronger than him.

"If I ever see you hit a woman like that again I might kill you, Tex. You hear what I'm saying? That woman has to be ma's age, what the fuck is wrong with you?"

"You fucked up now," Mrs. Martin says smiling, as she licks her own blood. Her white teeth turn burgundy. "You'd do better putting that gun to your head, than sticking around here for much longer. You'll see what I'm saying, Both of you. Your lives have been changed forever."

I couldn't take Mrs. Martin taunting Tex anymore, telling him about all of the things Mercury was going to do to him, once he found out. Stuff like snipping his nuts off and making Nigga stew. Real hardcore shit. So we threw a pink and white robe over her body, duct taped her mouth, and tied her to some pipes under the bathroom sink. They seemed to be sturdy and we kept walking back into the bathroom, just to make sure she hadn't gotten out.

We were in the master bedroom. I'm sitting on the bed, trying to figure out our next move while Tex is putting a fresh bandage on the stab wound on his arm. I guess after we fought, it came off.

"Why did you pull me into this shit, Tex," I ask him. "Just keep shit real with me. Is it because you don't love me?"

He looks back at me. "Why you coming at me with that punk shit?"

"I'm asking you a question," I yell stepping up to him. "I'm your brother and I don't want you beating around the bush nomore. Do you love me or not?"

"You know I do."

"Then why would you pull me in this, man? When you know I was almost out? I had a fucking chance."

"There you go making everything about you again."

"You don't even understand what's going on, Tex. You got Mercury's mother in the bathroom tied up." I point at the door. "I heard he killed his first victim at age six by pushing him off the balcony in his apartment. Just because he disrespected his mother. We don't rob people like that, Tex, we stay far away from 'em."

"Do you love me?" he asks me.

"You already know I do."

"Then why would you leave me alone with ma? To go to college? When you know the life we had coming up? Dane, I can't take care of her without you. What if somebody remembers what we did to them as kids? I think about that shit everyday."

"Don't talk like that."

"I'm serious. What if it happens? You gonna be somewhere in Texas, leaving me to deal with the shit all alone."

My phone rings in my pocket before I can answer him. I went out to get it from the car earlier, just before I pulled it into her two-car garage, to hide our ride. I take my cell phone out of my pocket and walk away from him.

"I gotta grab this call, Tex. Give me a second."

He shakes his head. "I swear whenever that bitch calls, you run. You might as well sew yourself onto the seat of her underwear." He walks out of the room.

"Stay away from the window," I yell at him. "And don't forget to check on her in about an hour." I answer the phone and sit on the edge of the bed. "Hello."

"Dane, is everything okay? You sounded bad when you ended the call with me and I've been worried."

"Asia, I gotta say something but I don't want you interrupting me when I say it. It's important that you listen because I don't know when I'll be able to tell you this again."

"Dane, you're really scaring me now."

"I know, and I'm sorry. But listen" —I swallow— "I know I don't treat you right all the time. It's not because I don't love you, or appreciate you. It's just that sometimes I don't always do the right things. But I need you to understand that there's nobody for me out there, Asia. Yeah I use to fuck a few dumb bitches, along the way, but not one of them stood next to you, and they all knew your name." I can hear her crying. "It doesn't justify my actions, I just want you to know how I feel."

108

"This sounds like the end and it will never be that for me. I don't know what's going on, but unless you're dead, I will always be by your side, Dane. I don't give a fuck what you're going through. If you gotta kill somebody, I'll put my hand over yours as you pull the trigger."

I laugh. "Why do I have a feeling you telling the truth?"

"Because you know that I am."

I'm smiling when I open my eyes, because I had a good night sleep. I don't remember my bed being this soft, and it feels like I'm at one of them upper class hotels. When I smell women's perfume, I sit up straight and look down at the floor. Before I caught a few hours of sleep, I told Tex, who was sleeping down there to watch Mrs. Martin while I grabbed a quick nap. Since the sun is shining into the room, I figure he let me sleep longer than I wanted to, and now it's the next day. The plan was to snatch two hours, and let him get a few too, until we figured out what to do with Mrs. Martin.

I hop up and walk into the living room. Tex is sitting on the sofa, with his head hanging over the back. Is this mothafucka actually sleep? What the fuck is this nigga doing? I walk around to the front of the couch and slap him in the face. He wakes up slowly. His eyes are low and I'm annoyed. I go into the bathroom and don't see her.

"Where is Mrs. Martin, Tex? Wake the fuck up before I steal you in your jaw."

"What...who is that?" he rubs the sleep out of his eyes.

I slap him again. "Nigga, wake up and tell me where Mrs. Martin is?"

"She's in the bathroom tub. Don't worry. I duct taped her to that fancy faucet she had in the tub. You probably didn't see her because I closed the shower curtain. Then I tied her legs with six ties and some rope I found in the cellar. Ain't no way she's getting out of that shit, man."

I immediately rush back to the bathroom. When I open the bathroom door I hear her talking on the phone. I snatch the shower curtain to the side. One of her arms is still bound, along with her feet. But the other hand is holding the phone in the tub. I immediately snatch it from her hand and hang up. Why didn't I peep the phone in the tub yesterday? So much was going on, that I didn't see it embedded into the wall. I thought it was a soap holder.

"Who the fuck was you talking to?" I look down at her. She doesn't respond. "I said who the fuck was you talking to?"

"You'll see. Don't worry, you'll see soon enough."

CHAPTER 14

TEX

My brother is driving and I'm in the backseat with the gun pointed to the back of Mrs. Martin's head. Her feet are tied together, and her left arm is tied to a hundred pound weight in the back seat at my feet, to prevent her from moving.

Dane gave me back my gun because he's driving, and she was starting to be a handful. Every so often she'd look at the scar on her face in the window, that I caused, and look back at me and frown. She could try it if she want to, and I'ma open up her head instead.

I gotta admit, when I pictured the plan in my mind it didn't go down like this. I just wanted Dane to fall back in love with getting money again, the way he use to. I figured if we took a big job, and made out on what we stole, he would see there wasn't no need for college. I guess I was wrong.

"Who was that, that knocked at the door last night," Dane asks her.

"I ordered Chinese food before you mothafuckas broke into my house." She says in a low voice. "It was the delivery man."

"Why didn't you tell us yesterday?" I ask her.

"You didn't ask." She looks out of the window to her right. "Just so you know, my son knows who you are now"— she laughs— "and when he gets finished with you, you'll wish he didn't."

Dane looks back at me and then at her. "So that's who you called in the tub?" Dane asks. "Your son?"

"What the fuck do you think," she laughs harder. "I raised that boy by myself you know? Since the day he was born I fed him meat, potatoes and blood. He's a man's man, and if there's one thing he knows in life, it's how to hunt and catch prey." She looks back at me. "And by prey I mean you two unlucky bastards."

"Your son ain't the only nigga who knows how to bust a gun, bitch," I tell her. "We got guns too."

"Tex, shut the fuck up with that dumb shit," Dane yells. "Let's not make the situation worse than what it already is."

"Oh...oh...I get it," Mrs. Martin says, "you the good one and you the bad one. Something like Cane and Abel. Well I don't know if you read the bible lately, but it ain't work out too good for them neither, just like it won't work out when Mercury finds both of you."

"Stop threatening us, lady," Dane yells. "Now I know it's fucked up that we broke into your house, and if I thought there was a way to let you go, and not be harmed I'd do it. But every time I consider pulling this car over and letting you out, you remind me why I shouldn't."

She shakes her head. "If you let me go without a plan, them green eyes of yours ain't the only things stupid. Your brain is too."

"Call your son," I say. "Call him now. I don't give a fuck."

She turns around and looks at me. "What you talking about?"

"Shut the fuck up with that dumb shit, Tex. Ain't nobody calling nobody."

"Why not? She says Mercury knows who we are already. Might as well talk to him and try to work some things out."

"This is a bad idea, Tex."

"I don't know if you figured it out, big bro, but we already in this shit deep. The least we can do is talk to this mothafucka and find out what's up with him."

"I feel like this is a bad idea, I'm telling you."

"And I feel like it's too late to do anything but make moves," I say.

"Now that you two mothafuckas have come to a conclusion, give me the phone. Let's call my boy and see what he has to say about this mess."

I dig into my pocket and hand her my cell phone. From the rearview mirror I see Dane looking at me. He's giving me the same look he did when I stole from Mrs. Dinkins purse as a kid, when I wanted money to buy a Superman comic book. He ain't talk to me for a week, until I raised enough money to pay her back. I'm getting the same feeling now. Like he's done with me.

"Son, I got some niggas who want to speak to you," Mrs. Martin says on the phone before looking at me. "Here he goes right here." She hands me the phone. "He wants to talk to you."

I take the cell phone from her. It shakes in my grasp, but slowly I put it to my ear.

"If you let my mother go, I swear nobody you love will be harmed." He says to me. "My offer expires in one minute."

"You talk like you the one who's running shit right now."

Silence. "What I gotta do, to get my mamma back?" he asks me.

I look at Dane, but he isn't looking at me.

"You can give me ten million dollars. We can start right there."

CHAPTER 15

MERCURY

Mercury is in the back seat of his Lincoln Limousine, trying to remain calm, even though his nerves were on edge. His beautiful driver Da Chun was behind the steering wheel, with all of her long black hair tucked under the chauffeur's cap she wore.

Mercury's huge body filled out most of the back seat, and although he was a big man, there wasn't a dude alive who could fuck with his dress code. Since he was filthy rich, he didn't bother visiting public clothing racks in search of garbs to cover his massive body. He chose to spend his time with his tailors, where they designed everything from his custom made crocodile slick bottoms, to the pink silk tie around his neck.

After getting off of the phone with Tex, Mercury considered his options. He grabs a cotton ball from the gold dish in the seat, and wipes off a few dirt particles that snuck up on his shoes.

"Since he has my mother do you think he has a mother too?" Mercury asks. "Of course he does," he responds to himself. "Everybody got a mamma, whether she's dead or alive. Now a daddy is a different story." He looks out of the window to his right. "I wonder how much he cares about her."

Those who didn't know Mercury would often be freaked out when he started talking to himself. But his close friends, family and even his driver, all knew this was his process. Shit, he talked some of his most violent crimes out before acting on them. Like when he killed his first child's mother, while she was giving birth to his daughter, when he was told that the baby was possibly not his. Even though a blood test later proved he was the father, and his child was motherless today, he didn't feel any remorse whatsoever.

Then there was the time he murdered his first cousin, Ryan on Thanksgiving Day. The incident was so trivial; some still couldn't understand what happened. From the most basic standpoint, Ryan made the mistake of telling Mrs. Martin that her turkey was dry, which resulted in an hour-long crying fit. Nobody but Da Chu saw Mercury who was sitting at the table, with his lips trembling, while he was trying to weigh the pros and cons of letting him live or die. The fight for Ryan's life was lost after

Mercury recalled how Ryan kissed his first girlfriend, during a game of Truth Or Dare that Mercury initiated. He killed him right there.

Yes...it was true, Mercury weighed every decision he made on the solo tip, believing the answers
to life's questions was internal anyway. He was going to do what he wanted.

"Da Chun, show me their faces," he says to
his driver. "I want to see what these niggas look
like."

Da Chun placed her index finger on the com-
puter screen within the dashboard of the limousine.
When the screen lit up, she logged onto the
Flickgram page and searched for Dane and Tex
Blake's pictures. After a little search, their pictures
pop up. Mercury leans forward and looks at their
green eyes. In every photo they are either posing in
the Weed-Mobile, or showing their mounds of weed
stashes.

He shook his head and sat back in his seat.
"What have you two niggas gotten yourself into?"
he asked himself. "You truly have fucked with the
wrong man's mother."

"I found their address earlier, from when you
mentioned their names the first time," Da Chun
says. "What do you want to do?"

"Take me to their house. Since they had the
pleasure of meeting my mother, it's time that I met
theirs."

CHAPTER 16

DANE

I'm standing outside of the car with my brother. We in a wooded area, some place in Maryland. I'm looking at him, trying to figure out who he is, because I don't recognize the nigga no more.

"Tex, why would you get on the phone and talk to slim 'bout his mother?" I'm pacing next to the car. "I'm not understanding you right now, so please clear it up. 'Cause the last thing we needed was this nigga to be tearing up the city trying to look for us."

"You heard the old bitch," he says pointing at her in the car. "She said he knew who we were. She said she told him in the bathroom. I got news for you, he already in this shit, Dane, the least we can do is get something our of it."

"You just destroyed everything, and you don't even know it." I sigh. "Maybe you don't give a fuck."

"By everything to do you mean your precious career as a college student? Is that what you're telling me? Because if you are, I don't give a fuck 'bout none of that, Dane, I don't. If that's wrong then so be it, but it's obvious that the only one you care about is yourself."

"You are so lost." I walk a few feet away from him, put my hands on my hips and look up into the blue sky. "Just gone."

"I'm gone," he points to himself. "I'm gone? At least I know who I am and where I come from, and I'm not letting you or some bitch named Asia, take that away from me. What about you though? Who are you now?"

"You just put everything on the line, Tex. Everything. Mama, Ray-Ray, Logan and us. You bet it all without even thinking of what you might lose or who you might hurt. Before you popped off and got on the phone with the nigga Mercury, I had a plan to get us out of this shit."

"And what exactly was your plan?"

"I was going to talk to Mrs. Martin, and try to get her to see—"

Tex starts laughing.

"What the fuck is so funny?"

"Remember when we were kids, and we were outside, and I stole Mrs. Nichols lemon cake from the window seal. She use to make them mothafuckas every Sunday for church, and they use to light up the apartment building. They made the hallway smell so sweet. She use to live on the bottom level, remember?"

"Get to your point."

"Give me a second"— he laughs putting one finger up— "From the day I could remember I always told myself that when I was tall enough to reach her window, I was gonna run off with one of them fucking cakes. All I needed was just a few inches and I was gonna be in there."

"Just like the movie *Life*."

"Except this wasn't no fucking movie, and it wasn't no whites only pies either. It was about me finally being able to do something for myself. It was wild too, because the summer before I actually did it, I was still short, and couldn't even reach the kitchen counter without your help. And then one day, well one summer, I sprouted."

"Sprouted huh?"

"Yeah," he nods leaning on the driver's side door. Mrs. Martin is still inside giving us dirty looks. "But then one Sunday Mrs. Nichols baked two lemon cakes, and I walked over to the window sill. I wasn't short this time, and I reached up, yanked that bitch and ran." He laughs.

"Yeah...and you got one bite in before her son broke your jaw, and put you out of the church choir for five months. You remember that? The fucked up part was that if you would've asked her, she would've given you what you wanted. It was wrong, man."

He's frowning. "Yeah...I remember. He got one in, but what you do though?"

"That ain't the point," I tell him.

"What did you do, Dane?"

I clear my throat. "I caught up with the nigga at gym glass, took a bat to his head and shattered every bone in his face, including the ones that he used to smile with."

"Exactly, you had my back, and I'm asking you to have my back now."

I sigh, and wipe my hands down my face. "Fuck."

"I know it's wrong, big bro, but at the end of the day we in this until the end now. There's no other plan that will allow you to walk away and not be involved in this shit. We either divide and you let me go at it alone, or we stay together and you help me beat it. I need your help, Dane. Don't you see what I'm saying? You got me or not?"

I look down at him. My heart is fucked up because if something were to happen to him, there would be no way I could live with myself.

"Is there anything else you gotta tell me?"

"What you talking 'bout," he says trying to laugh it off. "You know everything already."

"I'm serious, Tex. Are you being forthcoming about everything?"

"Forthcoming huh?"

"Nigga…"

"Okay, okay, I'm being *forthcoming* as you so eloquently put it." Tex laughs. "But, there is one thing." He pulls his pants down.

"What the fuck are you doing?" I look around.

Before I know it he has his dick out. "You see that shit?" he points at it.

"Tex, pull your fucking pants back up, nigga."

"Look at it. I know you ain't gay. I just need to know that whatever this shit is on my dick, it won't kill me."

Disgusted, and wanting to get this shit over, I took a quick look at it. I saw a small bump but it wasn't nothing serious. "That's a hair bump. Now pull your fucking pants up."

He does. "What the fuck is a hair bump?"

"Nigga, you shave every day, you got a hair bump, and it ain't even on your dick." I say frustrated. "Now, is there anything else, besides that disgusting shit you just made me witness? I'm talking about any more lies or dishonesty?"

"The only thing I held back on was the fully rolled bar I got in my pocket." He pats it. "I was gonna save it for us, for an emergency, but I figure we got a life or death situation going on right now."

"You right about that shit," I tell him.

For fifteen minutes, we smoke the bar and pass it back and forth. For that moment nothing else was going on in the world, and Mrs. Martin wasn't even in the car. We talked about how we made a snowman out of our next-door neighbor's son. We talk about the time Courtney the Clit let us run our first train on her for a dill pickle. And we talk about Marvin, the man who we thought for the longest time was our father.

"Let's get back in the car, man. It's time to handle this shit."

Tex lies down in the back seat and before getting in the driver's seat, I reach in the back to grab something. The moment I pull off Mrs. Martin lays into me. "I hope you two mothafuckas got a good high...a real good one at that. Now either kill me or let me go. I don't' give a fuck."

I'm so high, I feel like I'm floating behind the steering wheel. At the moment nothing she says bothers me. "Mrs. Martin, ain't nobody gonna hurt you. You good."

"Yeah, just relax," Tex says slapping her on the shoulder. "You keep being cool, and I have a feeling we gonna let you go."

For the next thirty minutes I drive in silence, with no special place to go. Just away from DC and Maryland. If my brother and Mrs. Martin are still talking I don't hear them anymore. I'm thinking about Asia, and how sexy her body looked the last time I saw it. I think about how she begs me to eat her pussy whenever she gets high. I love her so much, and I hope that one day I can be who she wants me to be, even though it's hard to see our future with all of this going on right now.

"I'm hungry, you hear me nigger," Mrs. Martin says.

When I look at her, she's staring in my direction. "What you just say?"

"You heard me mothafucka! I said I'm hungry."

"First off if you call me *nigger* again I'ma push you out of this mothafucka while I'm driving." She act like she ain't black.

"So the nice routine is over?" she asks me. "I knew it would be sooner or later. Now your as big of an asshole as your brother back there."

I don't answer.

"'Bout time you gave it to this bitch like she needs it," Tex says closing his eyes.

"Either take me to get something to eat or I'm going to make this ride uncomfortable," Mrs. Martin threatens.

"And how do you plan on doing—"

She's screaming so loud, my eardrums rattle. "Aight, calm the fuck down!" I yell. "I'm gonna let you grab something now." I quickly turn into a McDonalds, which was the first place I saw. Besides, after smoking that bar I'm kind of hungry too. I really wanna open a bag of Doritos, pore in some chili and cheese and call it a day, but I don't see a 7-Eleven around.

"What you want?" I ask her.

"Give me a Big Mac Meal, Dane," Tex interrupts.

I shake my head. "You have zero manners whatsoever."

I take Mrs. Martin's order, which is some nuggets and a diet soda. I get out of the car, and when I walk inside there's a large line. I'm in the restaurant for fifteen minutes, before my food finally comes out.

When I come back out I see Mrs. Martin holding a gun to my brother's face. From the window she's grinning at me, and my brother looks scared. It's like he reverted back to child hood days, and I feel helpless.

"Get in the car, and untie my legs and arm," she demands me.

Instead of doing what she asks, I drop the bag of food; release the gun from my waist that I stole from Tex in the backseat, and fire into the car window.

CHAPTER 17

MERCURY

Diane Blake was exhausted, and didn't feel like going to her doctor's appointment later. Not only was she not allowed to drive, neither Dane nor Tex had bothered to call her yet, to tell her who was picking her up and taking her.

Her mind floated around at all times. If she wasn't consumed with the idea, that someone was out to get her, she was thinking about her sons, and how awful a mother she'd been to them throughout the years.

Diane pretended like she didn't remember her sons' tumultuous childhood, whenever Tex wanted to speak about it, but she recalled everything.

When Marvin left her and he murdered Larry, she ran with a dangerous gang called the Gangster Devils. Although they sold drugs from time to time, their real hustle was murder for hire, and anybody could get it. At first Diane, with her beautiful face and wild spirit, would assist the gang by luring men to their deaths, with promises of sex. But when word got out that her kiss was deadly, she needed to find another hustle to help the gang, that's where her boys came in.

Faking injuries from gun shot wounds, to broken limbs, Dane and Tex would lead drug dealers or rich businessmen away from their cars and homes, only to be kidnapped and held for ransom. Because of their innocent faces and green eyes, over fifty men had met their deaths with their help. And although Diane tried to put those days out of her mind, Tex never got over the past, and feared one of their family members would soon find and kill them.

Diane sat Logan on the sofa, and placed a red plate full of chopped hot dogs in front of him, which was his favorite. When she heard a knock at the door, she opened it wearing her pink housecoat.

"Who you?" she asks the overweight, but handsome man before her.

"Well hello there, beautiful. My name is Mercury, and this is my driver Da Chun." Da Chun nodded and smiled.

Diane clutched the collar of her beast-ugly robe. "If you calling me pretty, either you blind or stupid. Now which one is it?"

"I'm talking about you," he points at her.

Diane looks behind her; just to make sure Ray-Ray didn't come back from the store early, and flash her nakedness like she had many times before to the mailmen when she stayed over.

"May I come in, ma'am? We are bearing gifts." Mercury looks behind him at Da Chun. She raises two grocery bags in her hands, tilts her head and smiles again.

"Well shit, he who has gifts is a friend of mine." Diane backs up and allows the killers into her home. Mercury walks up to the sofa and looks down at Logan who has a plate full of cold chopped hot dogs, with mustard and ketchup between his legs.

"Well hello there, little man, who are you," Mercury says leaning over toward the little boy.

"This is my neighbor's son," Diane replies. She didn't know why she lied, but for some reason, she felt inspired too.

Mercury eyes her suspiciously. "Well what's your name little guy?"

"Logan," he sings, popping a hot dog into his mouth.

"What a cool name? Who gave it to you?"

"My daddy."

Mercury hoisted the baby up, sat in the position he was in, and plopped the child on his lap. For fear the portly man would eat his food, leaving him with none, Logan placed the plate on his lap.

"Can I have one?" Mercury asks him.

"No," Logan responds flatly.

128

This strikes Diane as odd because Logan is normally so selfless and giving, that the family usually has to tell him to stop giving his food and toys away. But there was something about the man the child didn't like.

"Awe, come on, Logan, just one bite." Mercury opens his mouth so wide; the baby feared he would eat his face. Deciding it was best to part with his meat than his nose, Logan flings a hot dog chunk in his mouth. "That's a good boy." He eyes Da Chun, and then Diane. "Like I was saying outside, we brought groceries for you and your family. What did we get again, Da Chun?"

"Steaks and chops. And some fruits and vegetables I think."

"That's right...steaks and chops," he repeats. "You do eat meat in this house don't you?"

"If it got a heart beat, we fry it around here," Diane responds as she eyes his crocodile shoes.

"That's good to hear," Mercury chuckles. "Are you the lady of this family?"

"I am," she nods.

"Great, because I've been trying to reach Tex and Dane. We go way back and it's been such a long time since I've seen them. I know Dane had a birthday a month ago," he continues, remembering the picture he had on Flickgram of his birthday cake. "And I was unable to attend because I was out *of town. So I figured I'd come today. Anyway you know how life is, it gets in the way."*

"I believe lots of things get in the way. But you have to live as old as me to know that."

Mercury laughs. And then suddenly with a straight face he says, "Your sons...do you know where they are right now?"

Before she can respond Ray-Ray, with all of her ignorance, rushes inside of the house talking on the phone. "Bitch, I can't wait to see that shit. Ebony be popping a lot of smoke when she be on the block, but I bet she won't have shit to say now. Maybe after that we can go to the club since Tex is being trifling again and ain't answering my phone calls." When she sees there is company she says, "Girl, I'll call you back." She places her phone in her bag and says, "What's up, Ms. D! I ain't know you had company."

"We got company girl. He not here for just me."

Ray-Ray looks Mercury and Da Chun over. She snatches Logan off of the strange man's lap and says, "Who you?"

"I'm Mercury, and we are trying to find Dane and Tex, do you know where they are?"

"Well I don't know where Tex's cheating ass is right now, but if you looking for Dane you need to visit his girlfriend."

Mercury looks at Da Chun slyly, and then back at Ray-Ray. "You can help us with that?"

"Shit, for a bag of Black Gunion and fifty dollars, I'll tell your big sexy ass whatever you wanna know."

CHAPTER 18

TEX

The air is thick and muggy in *Princess G's Strip Club*. I'm way in the back, away from the crowd, within the darkness of the club. I'm sitting on a chair and Water Girl is on her knees, between my legs sucking my dick clean. Whenever we stop here to sell the shit we robbed from the houses to Tony Bones, I would make it my business to hook up with her. Ole girl don't play when it comes to the knob game and because of it she's my favorite.

I really needed to hook up with her tonight, after watching my brother kill someone in front of me, it fucked up my mind. I could tell in his eyes that he was forever changed behind that move, and I can't help but blame myself for that.

"You tasting real sweet tonight, Water Girl says looking up at me. "I love when you be like this." They call her Water Girl because she dances so hard she sweats.

I look down at her, while grabbing the back of her head. "I got different tastes or something?"

She looks up at me and stops sucking. "Kinda,"— she shrugs— "sometimes when you come in here though you be tasting like you fucked earlier in the day or something. What, you broke up with your girl?"

"Just suck my dick, WG. I ain't come in here for all that."

She looks at my shirt. "Why you got blood all on your shirt? You got hurt or something?"

"Just focus on your job, unless you don't want this money." I frown.

As she goes back to work I look up at my brother. He's in the front of the club, trying to sell the shit we got from our robbery. He looks stressed out, and part of me feels bad that I got him in this situation. But the other part of me feels like I made the best decision for both of us. He'll thank me later I'm sure of it.

When she runs her tongue along the shaft of my dick, I think I'm about to bust. Especially when she starts going quick. When she snakes her tongue into my pee hole, my legs tense up. "Don't hit me like that just yet, ma, take it up to the pole."

"You never could handle it when I licked that split," she giggles. "That's a signature move I couldn't teach if I tried."

I frown. "I don't have no split. I'm a nigga. That's the stupid shit you be doing that sets me off and makes me wonder why I fuck with you anyway."

"Damn, Tex, I'm just playing with you, why you getting all stupid and shit?"

"Stupid?" I push her off. "Get the fuck up."

"No…no…don't don't go. I need the money, Tex. You know I was only talking shit because you set me off. I ain't mean nothing by it, you know that. We cool. Plus I'm trying to get high later."

"Then do less yapping and more sucking. I got somewhere else to be."

I'm pawing the back of her head again when I see the club owner hand my brother some money. Dane looks toward the back of the club, and squints when he sees me. *Aw shit, this mothafucka is about to start tripping.*

Dane rushes up to me, looks down at Water Girl and back at me. "I know you not dumb enough to be back here getting your dick sucked, when we got business in the car." He's referring to Mrs. Martin's body, which is stuffed in the trunk. "Shawty, get your shit up and get the fuck out of here. My brother is done for the day." He throws her a fifty-dollar bill and she snatches it up.

Water Girl runs away, and I zip my jeans up. "Why the fuck you do that for? She didn't even make me bust!"

134

"Tex, are you that fucking gone, that you don't realize what's popping off right now?"

"Did you get the money from the stuff we copped? Because I'm tired of all this—"

I'm caught off guard by the blow I just took to the face, courtesy of my brother. I can't remember the last time he hit me that hard. If I had to pin point a time, it would be when I took his phone after he broke up with Asia last year.

After smoking a few bars on the playground, and going to eat at IHOP (International House of Pancakes) to help him get over her, he realized he couldn't find his phone. I convinced him that he lost it at the restaurant, and he was too upset to dispute. The truth was I kept his phone in the bottom of my dirty clothes hamper, and unplugged the house phone so he couldn't get her message.

Everyday he would check the voicemails and I would erase them before he could get to them. After awhile, he thought she hadn't called. I checked both messages Asia left him on his cell phone and the house phone, and knew she went out of town on some college tour. He was a zombie walking around the house, not eating or talking to anybody, and after awhile, he came to terms that it was over, or so I thought. When he went to her house preparing to ask her to marry him to take him back, I decided that I rather they be boyfriend and girlfriend than husband and wife. So I had to come clean.

To make shit worse, my brother gets bubble guts when he's going through the motions. So it wasn't until he was holding up the bathroom for the third day in a row, that I knocked on the door and handed him his cell phone.

At first he was relieved to have it, especially after I told him she called, but a second later he was angry—the angriest I saw him before now. He stole me in the face so hard that day that my eye was swollen for a week.

Tonight I'm tired of his shit. So I rub my jaw, and deliver him a blow so hard to the stomach that his mouth spreads open and spit flies out.

It's on now!

CHAPTER 19

DANE

"Ya'll gotta get out of here with this shit," somebody says behind me, as I gut punch Tex over and over.

At this moment he isn't my brother, I got more love for a nigga on the street, than I do for him right now. I just killed somebody for him, on the count of him having another gun that he purchased from Wico the other night. I realize that was probably what their side convo was for. How the fuck did she even get the gun? I'm done with my brother and tired of his selfish shit.

"I can't have this in my establishment," Tony says. "The both of you have to leave, now."

I don't respond. Instead I jab Tex's chin, sending him flying onto the dirty floor. When he get's up, a dollar bill is stuck to the side of his face and he tries to hit me. I shove him into the bouncer who walked up behind us.

137

"That's it, I'm sorry, Dane, but I can't have this shit in my club," Tony says firmly. He looks at the bouncer. "Aye, Mars launch these two mothafuckas outside of my spot."

I don't know how he did it, but Mars managed to lift me and my brother off of our feet, before tossing us out into the front of the club. It doesn't stop us from going at one another once we were out there, though.

We are shoving and pushing each other until Tex says, "Why he ain't wanna be our father? Why he walk out on us like that?"

"Fuck are you talking 'bout?" I shove him again, and he plunges into an Escalade. "I'm not trying to hear none of that shit right now. I'm tired of your recklessness, Tex. I'm done."

"Was we that bad?" he asks ignoring my questions. "Was we that awful that he didn't wanna love us?"

I'm breathing heavily, as I throw myself on the curb next to the truck Tex is leaning on. "He left because it wasn't his responsibility to take care of us anymore." I rub the knot I feel popping up on my cheekbone. "It ain't have nothing to do with me or you. I told you that a million times, and I don't understand why you wanna carry that load."

"Then why it don't feel like it's not my fault? Every day I wonder if there was something I could say to him, to get him not to leave, and the feeling never goes away."

"I don't know, man," I shake my head slowly. "I knew it was fucking with you, but I didn't know it was on this level."

"I didn't know either...'til now."

"Why now?" I ask him.

"Because I feel that I'm about to lose you too."

I stand up. I'm still mad so it's hard for me to look him directly into his eyes. So I stand a few feet in front of him. "Tex, you gotta know that no matter what happens, you'll always have me. But we men now, bro, not kids, and we gotta go after our own lives. It don't mean you'll lose me. Yes we may get older but it doesn't mean I won't be here when you need me either. But this shit you doing these days is making me feel like you don't give a fuck 'bout nobody but yourself."

"I fucked up big time didn't I?"

I look around and step closer to him, so that only he can hear my words. "We got a dead bitch in the trunk of our car, Tex. The mother of a well known killer. You can't get more fucked up then this if you tried." I back up a little to stare him down. "Plus I slumped a woman. You have no idea what I got going on in my mind right now. The guilt alone is enough to put me into zombie mode, but that's not going to help anything, so I gotta be strong for me and you. But I'll never be happy again when this shit is over."

He lowers his head and I can see tears roll down his face. "Hey, man it ain't' like—"

"Get the fuck off of me," he yells. "Don't put your fucking hands on me. I'm not no punk."

I raise my hands up in the air and back up. "What's wrong with you now, Tex?"

"Let's just go. I gotta get out of here."

"Whatever."

INSIDE OF THE CLUB

Tony, the club's owner, was on the phone behind the bar looking at Dane and Tex outside of the club. Although the music was loud, it wasn't stopping him from what he was about to do—snitch.

"Hey, man, ain't you looking for the Blake boys?"

"You know the answer to that already," Mercury says. "So are you telling me something I want to hear or are you wasting my time?"

"They're down here now."

There was a moment of silence. "If you can keep them there, I got five large waiting for you."

"I threw them out a minute ago, but with that invitation, I'll think of something."

"Good, I'll send somebody now."

CHAPTER 20

TEX

Hot water beat down on Ray-Ray's breasts, as she stood under the showerhead at her house. After we left the club, I took the car and decided to go to Ray's, while Dane took a cab to God knows where. I never thought I'd see the day, but Dane and me are no longer brothers and I gotta be cool with that.

I'm watching Ray, and she's doing all she can to turn me on. But the show is over at this point, because I just smoked a bar and the only thing on my mind is fucking and eating.

I push the shower curtain back and say, "Get out, Ray, and get into the bed." She turns the water off, and steps out of the tub, leaving a water trail on her gray carpet, all the way to the room. Before she makes it to the bed I change my mind. "Matta fact, don't even go to the mattress, drop that ass on the floor."

"You all the way live tonight, huh?" She wiggles to the floor. The water glistens off of her body and breasts. I walk toward the bed, and sit on the edge.

"I want you to suck it," I tell her.

She crawls over to me and says, "You don't have to tell me but once, baby. You know that."

I stroke myself to a partial thickness and she snatches my dick out of my hands. After stroking me five or six times, I'm as thick as I'm gonna get. She slides her tongue along the side of my stick, before rolling it over the tip. I took a shower earlier because if Ray-Ray can smell one thing, it's the scent of another woman. I didn't want her tripping off of Water Girl when it wasn't even like I got a chance to bust. Dane saw to that shit by that cockblocking move he made.

"Make it rain on that shit, Ray," I say looking down at her.

"Nigga, don't come at me like I don't know how to suck a dick"— slurp— "I'm the only bitch who can make you cum in under two minutes. Recognize me for who I am."

She's telling the truth but I always like to challenge her, because if I do it makes for a better experience.

"I think you falling off, Ray, I mean back in the day you use to be the shit on the blow job tip, but that was then."

"Oh yea?" Like a busy bee she gets down to business. One minute you see my dick and the next minute you don't because she swallows it whole.

"Got dayum, Ray-Ray," I say. "What the fuck you doing?"

She ain't responding to shit I'm saying. Instead she locks her tongue around the shaft of my joint and sucks so hard my balls rattle. Spit drizzles and oozes down my legs and her eyes roll into the back of her head.

It isn't long before my balls hum and the veins in my stick pulsate. "R-R-Ray"— I stutter— "hold up."

She doesn't stop, instead she continues to slurp, suck and gag on my dick. I'm done. I just wait for the feeling I know is about to arrive. Instead of fighting, I pawn the back of her head, and push into her face. Her eyes widen and at first it looks lie she's about to choke. Instead she winks, sucks harder and I cum into her throat.

"Awwww….shit, fuck," I moan.

Ray-Ray doesn't stop until every creamy drop is gone. "In case you were wondering, nigga"— she points at the clock— "that took one minute and thirty seconds. So don't fuck with me, you know how I do. My shit is crucial."

All the shit she's popping makes me want to fuck her really hard now. "Turn over."

"You want me to get on the bed?"

144

"Did I ask you to?" I frown. "Stay on the floor."

She flips over and raises that lopsided ass in the air. I crawl on top of her, and mount her ass. I slide my dick into her asshole, and kiss her on the back of the neck. She winds her waist and squeezes her walls again, making my dick feel like it's in a warm glove.

"Pound this shit, Tex!" She says winding into me. "Fuck me!"

"I see you talking that shit tonight." I lift up and hammer her ass harder. "I got shit for bitches like you."

"Then give it to me, nigga," she says. "It ain't like you don't know what I like. Make me feel something, and make it good."

In the past I have been known to hold back on Ray-Ray when I'm butt fucking her. I never pushed my entire dick into her, since I'm the reason her pussy is banged out. I try not to destroy the ahole. Truth is if I gave her everything I could, I know she couldn't take it. But tonight she's jawing a lot of shit and it makes me think I need to show her whose boss.

"What you waiting on, mothafucka. Fuck me r—"

Her mouth closes and her eyes widen when I slam all of my dick into her. She's trying to crawl away but I keep pulling her back. "Now talk that shit, bitch." I slam her harder and harder as I think about everything that's going on in my mind.

The bitch in the trunk outside. The argument I had with Dane. And Asia.

She looks back at me. "Tex…that…that kinda hurt."

"What you thought it was a game? You thought I was packing low weight or something? Think about that the next time you wanna pop shit. Think about how rough this dick feels."

"Tex, I don't think I can take it, baby. You gotta…you gotta—"

"I ain't gotta do shit but stay black and die."

I continue to fuck her until there's so much blood on the floor and on my dick that it looks like a crime scene. Since this is the second time I'm busting for the night, it makes it harder for me to cum so I take longer. Too bad the shit had to be in her ass.

"Please stop—"

"I'm about to cum, I'm almost there…fuckkkkkkk." When I splash into her, I fall on her back. She's crying a little and I sit up. "I'm sorry, Ray-Ray. I really am. I was up in my head."

She worms away from me. "Why would you do me like that?" she asks covering her ass.

"I got a lot of shit on my mind I guess. I really am sorry, baby."

"A lot of shit on your mind like what? You usually talk to me when you going through problems, Tex," she says sobbing harder. "You never do me like this."

"I know, and it was wrong." I want to tell her about the robbery and everything, but Ray has a big mouth, and might start telling everybody before we have a chance to correct the problem. "It's this nigga Mercury."

"You talking bout the dude who came to your house today? The drug dealer."

I lean into her. "What did you just say?"

"A dude came to your house today. He said he was a friend. He even took your mother to her doctor's appointment earlier and everything. I thought shit was cool. Why, is something wrong?"

"Are you saying, that this nigga got my mother? And you just telling me?"

"He ain't your friend?" she asks in a small voice.

"Ray, why wouldn't you tell me this when I came over earlier? We dropped off Logan to your cousin's house and everything! At no point did you think you needed to tell me that dude had my mother?"

"I'm sorry, baby. Did I do something wrong?"

All I see now is blinding rage.

CHAPTER 21

DANE

I'm laying in Memory's bed. She's on top of me. We just finished fucking and I wanted her to get up so I could take the condom off carefully, but she does this all of the time, and never wants to let me go.

Memory is a cute redbone, short chick with long black hair. She's exactly the opposite of Asia and I like it that way. Back in the day I was only attracted to dark skin girls with big asses and small facial features like Asia. But I realized that they made me feel guilty because they reminded me too much of her.

When me and my brother got into it earlier tonight, I could've called Asia and went over her house, since she lives alone, but she asks too many questions, and I don't feel like talking right now. Most of the time Memory is easy going, although she has a sneaky side too that I haven't figured out yet. I been dealing with her for months now, and I never had a major problem, she seems to be low-key and laid back.

"What's on your mind, Dane?" she asks me. "You look like you somewhere else."

I squeeze her ass cheeks. "What you need to be asking is what's on my dick. Because right now it's this funky pussy."

She giggles. "Yuck, you nasty," she says slapping my chest. "I'm serious. You look like you got a lot on your mind. You and Asia didn't get into it again did you? I saw how upset she was when she came to my house the other night, and saw you here. The last thing I want is for ya'll to be fighting over me."

"What I tell you about saying Asia's name?" I frown. "Didn't I tell you I don't want you talking about her? What we do, we do and it's as simple as that."

"Damn, nigga, you act like I'm gonna call her up or something. Ain't nobody fretting nothing about your little girl friend. Trust me, it's not that deep and it never will be over here in Baltimore. Keep all that extra emotional shit in DC please."

She is talking a lot of slick shit. "Get off of me." She's about to jump up quick, but the condom is still on my dick. "Slowly, Memory." She jumps up fast anyway. "What a stupid bitch."

149

"I'm done with you"— she stands naked across the room—"Don't ever come back here again. I'm serious this time."

I take the condom to the bathroom and flush it down the toilet. When I'm done I go back into her bedroom. "If you don't want me back over here, you got it." I get dressed. "Your pussy expired anyway."

"My pussy expired?" She repeats walking up to me. "Nigga, is that why you be beating down the beltway from DC to Baltimore to get at this shit? Because it expired? I doubt that very seriously, sir, thanks for the lies anyway. If anybody expired it's you."

As she screams and rants I feel a little guilty. Although I'm not feeling her right now, the real reason my mind is gone has nothing to do with her. When I first got over here, I took a nap because I was so stressed out over Tex. Apparently I was having a nightmare when I didn't realize that I was even dreaming. In it I had a vision that my girl was murdered, and it rubbed me the wrong way.

When I woke up and saw Memory next to me, part of me felt bad, because if something did happen to Asia, and I'm in this bed, it would crush me.

With all that said, no matter what I got going on, Memory had been drama free and I owed her more than this. She never gave me grief, and minded her tongue when Asia called and read her the business. Although I'm sure it will be my last time dealing with her, I don't want to bounce on bad terms.

"…so you don't ever have to worry about me again, Dane."

"I'm sorry," I say.

"What?" She folds her arms over her chest.

"I said I'm sorry." I grab both of her hands. "Look, I got a lot of shit on my plate, and I guess it slid off and onto yours. It don't give you the right to come at me like you did neither, but I can understand why you would be mad."

She smiles. "Boy, you were trying to give me a heart attack with the way you were talking to me. I'm not use to having men disrespect me like that. Getting me all riled up and shit for nothing."

"You right, and I'm never gonna come at you like that again, but I gotta bounce. Okay? There's some things with my brother that I gotta clear up."

"I understand, do what you gotta do"— she smiles and wipes her hand down my cheek— "Whenever you're ready I'll be here. Your invitation is open again now."

"You got that, ma," I reply, knowing I'm never coming back.

I throw the rest of my clothes on and slip into my Jordan Bred's. When my wallet falls off of the table, on the side of the bed, I pick it up. When I do I see a pin. A stickpin. I don't know what made me look at the condom wrapper next, but I do and immediately something looks off. When I zero in on it closely, I see what I'm looking for. Right in the center of the letter 'O' on the Trojan wrapper, I see a pinhole. I grip it in my hand tightly and walk over to her.

"What's wrong now, Dane?" She backs away a little.

I ball it up. "What the fuck is this?"— I throw the wrapper into her face— "don't tell me this shit? You sticking holes in the middle of condoms trying to trap a nigga?"

She immediately starts crying. "I'm sorry, Dane, I just wanted a baby so badly. I'm in this house all by myself and I'm tired of being alone. I wasn't even going to come at you like that."

This bitch is bionic. Who does some crazy shit like that? "But I don't want no baby with you, Memory. I don't want a kid with nobody but my girl."

"And you're telling me that after you fuck me," she says putting her hands on her hips. "It ain't like you got no good sperm anyway, clown. I been sticking them condoms in that wrapper ever since we started fucking and I still ain't got pregnant."

"If I'm such a clown, why you wanna have a baby by me?"

"Because I wanted my child to have them green eyes, it ain't like you worth nothing else."

What this bitch trying to say, that I can't have kids? That my sperm is as good as milk? "Don't ever call me again, Memory. If you come near me or mine I'ma hurt you."

"We'll see about that."

When I leave out of her apartment building, I see my brother approaching. What this nigga want now, and how did he know I was here?

CHAPTER 22

MERCURY

Mercury walked downstairs of the basement in the grocery store he owned, with Da Chun following him. Mrs. Blake sat tied up on a wooden chair, and one of Mercury's ties were tied in her mouth, holding her tongue down. Behind her were three of his men, who were waiting on orders on what to do with her next. She was visibly shaken and afraid for her life, and she should be.

"Has anyone called yet," Mercury asks one of his men, over her head. It was as if she wasn't even there.

"No, we've been sitting by the phone," he replies.

"This doesn't make any sense," Mercury says looking down at her. "Why wouldn't they call?" He observes Diane's shivering body. "Do your children love you?" He asks although he's talking to himself.

"Don't hurt me," she mumbles. "Please."

"They're probably waiting to see if I'll give them the money they are asking, for the return of my mother first," he responds to himself, ignoring her comment. "Maybe they don't think I'll hurt her"— he eyes Diane again—"if they do, they don't know me very well"— he looks at his man—"Are you sure the phone is on?"

"Yes, sir"—he raises the phone into the air— "we have full signal strength and everything. Still no call."

Mercury looks down at his shoes. He hated himself for never considering the angle that his mother could be kidnapped, let alone by two idiots. In his mind people weren't stupid enough to fuck with his mother, but he was wrong.

"Find that bitch," Mercury demands.

"Who, sir?"

"The one I left alive to give the message. Had I known they didn't care about their mother, I would've snatched her instead. Get the kid too, I have a feeling that's his son."

"Not a problem, sir."

Da Chun whispers into Mercury's ear. Mercury observes her and smiles. "Let's see where this Asia bitch is also, the one the girl talked about. If we get the both of them, I'm sure they'll be willing to hand over my mother then."

Mercury turns to walk up the stairs.

"But, sir," the soldier says. *"What do we do about her?"*

"Kill that bitch. I'm not running a babysitting service."

CHAPTER 23

DANE

I know Tex has something to tell me, while we sit in the car, him behind the steering wheel and me in the passenger's seat. I can tell by the look on his face that something is on his mind. I wish he just get it over with. He promised me earlier that he didn't have no more secrets, and I hope he didn't lie about that too.

"What you gonna take up in college?" he asks me. "You never told me before, and I didn't ask you."

I sigh. "I got a scholarship for academics, with a major in journalism."

He looks at me. "I never knew you wanted to be no reporter."

"You never asked."

He nods. "I want you to know that this shit is all my fault. I know you know it already, but I wanted you to hear it from me. I wish I can take back the shit I did, but I can't."

"Tex, tell me something I don't know already. Like what you really want."

"No, I really mean—"

"Tex, I'm tired of the fucking games, man. You don't even like Baltimore, yet you show up here just to tell me that this shit is your fault, and ask me about my college career"— I pause— "stop fucking around and tell me what's going on. Don't forget we got a body in the trunk that's going to start stinking in a minute."

"When I said it was my fault, I mean it's really my fault. And before we split up, I want you to know everything, starting with why I picked Mrs. Martin's house."

My jaw tightens. "I'm listening."

"You know how we run the schemes."

"Yeah...we find out who gonna be gone, based on them dropping off their dogs, and we rob their crib. Again get to the point."

"Well Mrs. Martin didn't drop off Heidi. That's not how I made the decision to hit her house."

"What you mean?"

"I knew she was home, man. I'm telling you I knew she was going to be there when we went in."

I feel like somebody just punched me in the stomach, and I can feel my forehead moisten. "Are you telling me, that when we walked up in that woman's house, you knew she was home? And you let me go in there with you anyway? Is that what you saying?"

"I followed her, while you was trying to reach Asia on the phone. Before seeing Mrs. Martin, I was gonna go home. And I said fuck it, let's hit her house. I took it as a sign."

I can feel my temples throb, and I clench my fists. "You ruined my life, over what, Tex? Why did you do this shit? Everything you wanted me to get behind I supported, and was always in your corner! You couldn't be in mine for one moment?"

"I wasn't thinking. I wanted to know how far you would be willing to go for me. I wanted to see if it would be me or Asia, and you chose me. You might not know it but since she's been in the picture it hasn't been that."

As he's talking to me, I'm thinking that I don't know my brother anymore. I'm thinking that I never knew him. And then something pops in my mind. "You saw me take the gun from the backseat right? Before I went inside McDonald's?"

"Yea," he nods.

"You knew I would kill her. Didn't you?"

"Yea."

"How did you know she had the gun?"

"I pulled it on her."

"You had another one?" My head is thumping.

"Yea."

"And you let her take it from you. What if she would've fired on you?" When I see the twinkle in his eye I have the answer to my question. "You didn't care. It meant more to you, to see what I was willing to do for you."

I think about crashing his chest in, but I'm tired of fighting him. He's done so much shit to me, that I can't think anymore. I gotta get away from him. I don't care if I go to jail or not, I will never fuck with my brother again. I put that up to God.

Before I leave, I need to ask one last question. "Why you telling me this shit now?"

"Cause he got mamma."

I lean in. "W-who got mamma?" I stutter.

"Mercury."

"You wasted all of this time, telling me about the dead bitch in the trunk, when this nigga got our mother? T-Tex, what...why didn't you tell me this first?"

"I wanted you to know everything, Dane. I'm done lying to you."

"You said that shit before," I yell.

"I'm being real now."

I sit in the seat and look into the darkness outside. I see a lady walking her dog, with a smile on her face and I wonder who she's talking to. Maybe it's her sister, or brother, and maybe life for them is sweet. Maybe if she knew what I was feeling for someone I considered family, she would be disgusted by me.

"When you was a kid I always had your back, Tex, I put you before me, even when I knew I shouldn't. You were my kid brother and I wanted to protect you. I didn't want you thinking that I would abandon you like pops did us, because I knew how important that was to you. Throughout our entire life, you have proved to me that it was all about you and nobody else. Well I'm done, son. I don't give a fuck what happens to you anymore."

"What you saying?"

"I'm saying we not brothers no more. I'm saying that I'm out here by myself, even if I die, and you better recognize the same thing too."

"You don't mean that shit," he says to me. I open the car door. "Dane, you don't mean that shit right?" I slam the door. "Dane," he continues to yell from the car. "Dane!"

CHAPTER 24

TEX

I just watched my brother walk away. I'm driving the car, on the way to Ray's, smoking a week old bar I had in my glove compartment. It's hard, and old, not even good, but it'll give me what I need right now.

When I make it to Ray's house I look around her neighborhood, jump out and run into the house. I don't know who's watching her or me, which is why I'm here. When I walk into the living room, she's there with my son, and feeding him hot dogs. *Again.*

"When you gonna start giving him real food instead of bullshit," I ask. "Out of all of the junk food in the world to feed him, you can't part with hot dogs just once?"

"What do you want?" she rolls her eyes, and I feel bad when I see how bad her left eye is swollen. When she didn't tell me that Mercury had our mother, before we had sex, I made a mistake and hit her in the face. "We don't want you here, Tex. Just get out."

Not paying her any mind, I take my son from her, and he wraps his arms around my neck. "Hi, daddy."

"What's up, little man?" I rustle his hair. "You eating hot dogs again?"

"That's all he likes," she says. "And I like to feed him what he likes."

He tries to stuff a hot dog in my mouth and I turn my head. "I'm good, lil man"— I look down at Ray who is sitting on the sofa with her arms crossed over her chest— "You can't be here, Ray, it's not safe. That's why I came, so stop looking so crazy and come on. It's time to bounce."

"Who am I running away from?" she says continuing to look at the TV.

"Are you really this stupid or just high?"

"Well I'm not stupid. You hit me and you fucked me in my ass to the point where it bled."

I place my hand over Logan's right ear. "In front of our son though?"

"He heard worse, Tex. I mean if you have a problem with me, why do you keep fucking me? If you hate me so much just leave me alone. It's obvious I'm not smart or cute enough for you."

"What you talking 'bout?"

"Bird told me you fucked her again, when I left out to make your food the other night."

What a stupid bitch. I'm done with Bird now.

"Ain't no need in your lying about it, Tex, because I already knew that you would do that shit."

I'm confused. "If you thought I'd do it why did you leave out the room?"

She sighs. "Because I love you, and if the only way I can be with you is like that, then it's what I gotta do."

I sit the baby down. "Look, I know I don't treat you right all the time."

"None of the time," she says cutting me off.

"Whatever the fuck, you know what I'm trying to say"— I pause—"I know we don't have the best situation but it's ours, and I don't want anything to happen to you. If you want to fuss with me tomorrow 'bout this, then it's all good. For now it's time to bounce."

She sniffles. "So where we gonna go?"

"Get dressed, I'm gonna drop you over your cousin's. Don't call your dumb ass friends or nobody else and tell them where you are. It's important, Ray-Ray, because I don't know what this nigga might be willing to do, and right now he has my mother. Now hurry up."

"Okay." She runs around the house getting Logan's clothes.

I sit with Logan in the living room. "Hey, lil guy." He smiles and my heart skips. "You know daddy loves you right?"

He nods. "Yes."

"You gonna be a good little boy over your cousin's?"

He grabs his toe. "Yes."

"Good, and I'll bring you something back too."

"Where uncle Dane?"

"He not here."

"I want to see him," he pouts.

"Maybe later, lil man." I sigh. "I wouldn't mind seeing him too."

"I got all of his things together," Ray says coming back into the living room. "You ready?"

"Yeah." I stand up.

"Before we leave I gotta give you something"— she sticks her hand into her pocket and pulls out a sheet of paper— "before you left, I forgot to give you this number, because you hit me. Anyway the guy said that you or Dane could call him about how your mother's appointment went. He said he won't tell anybody but you."

I just dropped off Ray and Logan at her cousin's. The moment they were in the house, I called Mercury to get the status on ma. "So you finally called," he says to me.

"Where the fuck is my mother, nigga?" I ask him. "Huh? Do you realize what I will do to this bitch if my mother's hurt?" I'm so serious, that I forget Mrs. Martin is already gone.

"I'm glad you finally got around to calling me, but you can kill the threats. Before this night is over, if my mother is not returned to me, unharmed, I will kill everybody you and your brother know and love. Do you hear me? You have one hour to meet me behind the old shopping center on Bladensburg road. Next to the Laundromat. You and your brother better be there." He hangs up.

The moment the call is over, I immediately think about Asia. I don't like the bitch, but I know my brother loves her. If something were to happen to her he wouldn't be able to take it. I sit back in my seat and try to remember where she lives.

Before going anywhere, I remember I have to do something. I take a card out of my pocket. It's the card belonging to officer Stern. On it I see a cell phone number so I dial it. The phone rings once before he finally answers.

"Stern."

"Officer Stern, this is Tex Blake. I want to talk to you about the robberies."

"What about it?"
"I want to confess to the crimes."

CHAPTER 25

MERCURY

Mercury sat outside of Asia's house, in the backseat of a jet black Navigator. Da Chun was driving and to the left and right of him were Sammy and Torrent, his goons. From his viewpoint he could see Asia getting dressed in her window, and his jaw hung. She was stunning. The white lace underwear set she wore showcased her silky chocolate skin, and she looked flawless.

"Go in and get the girl," he tells them.

"You still want us to kill her?"

He looks at the window again, and takes in her beauty. "Bring her to me if you can, if not, do what you have to do to get her out of there, dead or alive"— he paused— "Close the curtains before doing anything, I don't want anybody seeing anything from out here."

"Got it, boss."

The truck's doors opened and they went to handle business, while Mercury remained and thought about his mother. After everything was resolved, and she was home, he had no intentions of allowing her to live in that house alone a day longer. He already secured a beautiful peace of property in West Virginia, with a large water fountain in the backyard. From her bedroom she could see an expensive garden with the most beautiful colored flowers the mind could imagine. It was time for his mother to sit back, entertain close friends and family and enjoy her life.

After about fifteen minutes of waiting on his men, he noticed they hadn't returned.

"What's taking you so long?" he asks himself. "I know you can handle her. She can't weigh more than a buck fifty."

"You want me to go check on them," Da Chun asks, hearing his one-on-one conversation.

He shakes his head softly and eyes the window again. "No, but you can come with me."

Mercury observed his surroundings before going inside. From what he could see no one seemed to be looking at the house. Both of them slid out of the truck and walked into the popped front door. Once inside, to Mercury anyway, things looked smooth.

"Something doesn't feel right, boss," Da Chun tells him in the living room. "Why don't you go back *and wait in the truck"— she pulls out the .45 tucked on the inside of her jacket— "I'll take things over from here."*

"I'm not going anywhere," he replies, leading the way toward the back of the house. "I need to see for myself what the fuck is going on."

As he walks down the hallway, he observes the pictures on the wall. Asia is posed in most of them along with an older woman. He figures she's Asia's mother, and wonders where she is now.

When he finally makes it to the only closed door in the hallway, he whips out his .45 and pushes the door open, aiming his weapon inside. He couldn't push the door open fully, without tripping over Sammy's body. He places his finger on his neck, seeking a pulse despite knowing he was gone. Bullet holes were riddled throughout his torso. When he looks across the room, he sees Torrent's body slumped over the edge of a chair. Bullet wounds are everywhere on him too.

Despite the grim situation he can't help but smile. Even though he sent two grown men to take care of her, she switched the tables around. Asia proved to be as dangerous as she was beautiful. Still, he needed to get his hands on her. For one he needed her as collateral to get back his mother, and he wasn't sure who else she was willing to kill.

"Come on out, Asia, you took two of my men, but I won't be as easy. I've been firing a gun since I

was five years old,"—he looks under the bed—"and Da Chun over here sleeps with her weapon at all times. Needless to say we're both pros." He looks into the closet. "Unlike my men, God rest their souls, it won't be as easy." He looks around the quiet room. "So come out, now."

After thirty more seconds of silence Da Chun says, "I don't think she's in here."

Although he hated to admit it he says, "Me either. The question became where did she go?

They went through the house, until they happened upon the kitchen. On the floor they saw a trail of blood leading towards the back door. One of his men must've shot her. Guns aimed, both of them dipped into the backyard, on a quest to find Asia. They rushed toward the gray shed, and looked inside, but she wasn't there. They looked inside the empty doghouse and she wasn't there either. It was as if she vanished.

"Let's go look for her," Mercury says.

They dip to the truck. When they see a stray German Shepard dog, believing it belongs to Asia, Mercury instructs Da Chun to ride on the side of it. The dog growls at the truck, and Mercury raises his weapon and shoots it dead, before instructing Da Chun to pull off. Thirty minutes passed and still they could not locate her.

Finally Mercury pulls out his phone and calls Tex. "I got the girl Asia, and I'm coming for Ray-Ray next."

"If you hurt her I'll torture—"

"You not gonna do shit but what I tell you. Now I expect to see you at the location discussed, if not, I'm gonna be burying your people for the next few days to smoke you out. And, then I'm killing you."

CHAPTER 26

DANE

I'm sitting in a stolen Caprice, outside of my house. Normally I don't steal cars, but tonight is an exception. I can't trust my car to get me around while I search for my mother, and make sure she is okay. Part of me wants to go to the police, to get their help to bring her home, and another part knows I must handle this in the streets.

I'm just about to go inside my crib, to see who's there, when I see a nigga in a black hoodie going around the back of the house. I grab the gun I took from Tex, and sneak behind him before he makes it to my back door. I rush toward him, tackle him to the ground and turn him over to point my gun into his forehead. I'm about to blow his scalp back until I see my baby's face.

I tuck the gun in the back of my pants. "Asia…what the…why are you back here?"

"I've been shot"— she removes her bloody hand off of the side of her stomach— "I need help, Dane. Please, or I'm probably gonna die."

Her eyes close and my heart dips. I get off of her, lift her up and rush her to the car. "Don't die on me, baby." When I look down at her, her eyes are still closed. "Asia, are you hearing me, don't die on me. Wake the fuck up, you can't be going to sleep."

She opens her eyes as I'm laying her on the back seat. "Don't worry, I won't die on you." Her smile is weak and melts my heart. I know she's trying to be strong for me, but she doesn't have to. "Just hurry up and get me out of here, before I won't have any control."

I dip behind the steering wheel and speed away from the house. When I remember that I'm speeding and am in a stolen car, I take it down just a notch. "Talk to me, baby"— I look at her from the rearview mirror— "Asia, talk to me so I can make sure you stay up."

"I'm up"— she moans— "just get me to the h...hospital. Please."

"I am, but I need you to tell me something I wanna hear. Who did this to you." She moans some more, and doesn't respond. "Asia, who did this to you?" I yell louder.

"I don't know, it was two big men. They came into my house." She says in a tiny voice. "They kept telling me to come with them and I didn't wanna go.

174

I don't know what they wanted from me, I don't have any money."

"And they let you get away?"

She giggles lightly. "I put so...so many holes in them with my mamma's gun, that they were whistling when I left."

Damn I love this bitch. "How you get away?"

"Went out my backyard, and hid in the dog pin with my neighbor's dog, a house over. I let my dog out since I knew they would probably...OUCH!" she screams. "I knew they would probably hurt him. What do you think they wanted, Dane?"

I know that it was either Mercury or his men, and I feel bad for getting her involved in this shit. It's making me hate Tex even more. "Don't worry about all of that, be easy, baby, don't talk too much now."

"You gonna marry me, Dane?" she sighs. "I'm not sure, but I got a feeling that this was somehow related to you. Am I right? The least you can do is be my husband."

I chuckle a little. Leave it to my bitch to figure me out and ask me to marry her during a time I can't say no. "You know I'm going to be your husband and you my wife, but I need you to stay alive and ask me again. The right way. Okay?"

"We gonna have babies? I always wanted lots of babies, so I could name one of them after my mamma."

I think about what Memory said. If she had been trying to trap me for the longest, and she didn't get pregnant, maybe I couldn't have any kids. No matter what I felt, now was not the time to tell her that.

"You make it out of this, and we can have as many kids as you want."

"You promise," she says moaning louder.

"I promise."

When my cell phone rings I answer it, even though the number is blocked. "Who is this?"

"It's me, Tex. Look, man, I know you said you don't wanna hear from me anymore, but I gotta tell you something."

I hang up and throw the phone into the passenger seat. When he continues to call, I wonder if he has any more information on mama, so I answer it. "What the fuck do you want, nigga? Make it quick."

"I wanted to tell you, that I'm sorry. I keep thinking about how close we were just a week ago, and how far apart we are now. I don't like this for us, man, we brothers. I know you always forgive me, and I know I always fuck up again, but I need to know if you will forgive me one more time. I don't want anything from you, bro, nothing at all this time. Just your forgiveness."

Just hearing his voice is causing my temples to throb, especially with my bitch doing bad in the back seat. Forgiving him is the last thing on my mind. "You got mamma?"

"No…I'm trying to—"

"If you don't got mama there ain't no way I could ever forgive you. Not this time."

I think about telling him that I have Asia, and that she was shot, and that it was all his fault, but I don't bother. It ain't even worth it for me. He ain't worth it for me anymore. Instead I end the call, throw the phone in the seat and continue down the road.

When I hear a sound from my baby in the backseat, like she's taking her last breath, I panic and the car swerves. "Asia…Asia! Answer me! Answer me please!"

CHAPTER 27

TEX

When I pull behind the building, and see Mercury's limousine, and a Chinese bitch standing outside of it, I think about turning around. *You started this shit and now you have to finish it. If you turn back now, all he's gonna do is go after your brother.* I decide to man up and push forward.

Dane's right about me, from the beginning I was fucking up, always causing him problems where there shouldn't have been none. It was time for me to answer to this situation. So I pull up beside the limousine, park and hop out. The moment my car door closes, two large men rush over to me, and run their hands over my body.

"What the fuck is this shit about?" I tell them. "And where is Mercury?"

"Shut the fuck up, nigga. We asking the questions around here." When they are done, one of them turns around and yells, "He's clean."

The Chinese chick opens the back door leading to the limousine and Mercury's big ass roles out. As hot as it is out here, this mothafucka is wearing a full gray suit. He cracks his knuckles, and approaches me. I'm thinking he's about to hit me, or even shoot me judging by the way his eyes lower.

Instead of being intimidated I say real calmly, "Where's my mother?"

"Easy," he says stepping up to me. "One thing at a time." He looks me over again from the top of my head to my feet. He's bigger and taller than I imagined. Like a giant. "You know what, as much shit as you popped over the phone, I figured you'd be a little taller than you are. You ain't nothing but a little runt, who's out of his fucking league."

I smirk. "Big things come in little packages." He laughs and again I ask, "Where the fuck is my mother?"

"Where do you think she is?"

My heart rate increases. I know immediately what he's about to say before he says it. Even if he lies and tells me she's alive, I know it's not the case. I think about that dream I had awhile back, the one with the white house. It finally dawned on me. When I walked into that house, with mamma and Larry, the house signified my death. Signified the end and Dane staying outside of the house meant he would live.

"Your mother is fine, and once I get mine, I will take you to her. Now, where is my mother?"

I swallow and look up at him. I fix my mouth and say, "Dead." The moment I say the words I feel light. Like I've made a big mistake.

"Fuck you mean dead, nigga?" He roars.

"Is there any other definition for dead? She's gone. She's eliminated and you will never see her alive again."

He looks at his men, and I can see him trembling. "Check this nigga's car."

This is the moment I knew would be coming. After they search the inside of the car they yell, "She ain't in here!"

He looks at me. "Where is my fuckin' mother?"

"She's inside," I smile. "Check the trunk."

His face seems to puff up and his eyes widen. "On everything, if my mother is in that car you gonna—"

"She's in here," one of his men says. "I-I'm sorry, man," he stutters.

"Is...is she alive?"

"No."

"You come to this meeting, with my mother in the trunk of your car? And think you gonna live?" I see a tear roll down his face but he acts like it's not even there. "Do you know what kind of mother she was? What kind of person you killed?" He grabs my

180

throat and squeezes. My oxygen supply shortens. "You think I'm a joke?"

"Who said I wanted to live"—I smile— "and just so you know, my brother didn't have anything to do with this shit. Your mother had been getting on my nerves since the moment I picked that bitch up. She was getting hard to listen to, so I got rid of her. You should know too, she fought to the death. You came from a thoroughbred but eventually I took her out."

He steps back and says, "Immediate death is too good for this piece of shit. Torture his ass until ya'll can't take it no more. Then I want so many holes in this nigga he'll turn to sand."

I hear the click of many guns first. I raise my arms, and look up into the night sky. I think about my brother, and how much I want him to succeed in life. "I hope you can forgive me now, Dane."

CHAPTER 28

DANE
(FIVE MONTHS LATER)

I'm sitting on my nephew's bed removing his navy blue tie. Ever since we buried my mother and brother five months ago, and he wore his first one to the funeral, he wanted to wear one even if it was the only thing he had on. We are living in off campus housing, for Prairie View A & M University, which is paid for in our scholarship fund that we have. I was able to convince Ray-Ray to let me keep him, because nobody knew where Mercury was. I needed Logan to stay with me for his protection.

I'm not gonna lie, it was nice getting away from DC, back at home I have two many memories.

"It's time to go to bed, Logan." I pull back the covers and put him inside. "We going to the amusement park tomorrow though. You ready to get on the roller coasters? And eat that cotton candy you like?"

"I can't wait," he says clapping his hands together. "I love cotton candy, and funnel cakes."

Suddenly he seems sad again. He does this a lot. A smile will be on his face and suddenly it would be wiped off and he'd start crying. I know he misses his father.

"Say your prayers before you go to bed, lil man, or you not going."

He slams his eyes shut and sings, "Now I lay me down to sleep, I pray the lord my soul to keep, if I should die before I wake, I pray the lord my soul to take."

"Good, boy." I rustle his curly hair. He seems sad again. "So what's wrong now?"

"Can I talk to daddy again?" he pouts. "Before I go to bed?"

"You can talk to daddy anytime you want, man, go ahead."

He looks up at the sky and says, "I love you, daddy"— he opens his arms wide— "this much. I'm going to be a good little boy at the amusement park too. And me and uncle Dane gonna have so much fun."

I laugh. Sometimes when he talks about Tex too much, it brings me down. "Aight, little man, that's enough, it's time to go to sleep for real."

I stand up and move toward the door."

"Uncle Dane…"

"Yeah, lil man."

"I love you too."

"I know, homie. I love you back."

When I walk out of his room, I see Asia sitting in the living room. Instead of going there, I go into the bathroom. I close the door and slide to the floor. I can smell the scent of bleach from the toilet that Asia cleaned earlier. Since we moved in together, there wasn't a time I can think of that she didn't prepare a hot meal, and keep a clean house. She's cool to live with, but sometimes I feel trapped. Like I need my own space.

I look up at the ceiling. When my brother died, it fucked me up how I ended our last call. I can't stop thinking about when we were coming up, and the day our lives changed when we found out the man who we thought was our father wasn't. But more than anything, I can't forget how I treated him when he asked for forgiveness. We was supposed to stay together. We was supposed to stay brothers.

"Tex, I know you up there, doing everything you can to get on God's nerves." I laugh. "You probably somewhere, smoking a bar with Tupac and Biggie." I look down at my hands. "Or even Uncle Larry." A tear rolls down my face and I wipe it away. "I just wanted to tell you, that I'm sorry, man, for not being there when you needed me the last time we spoke. I know I never spoke to you before now, but it was just too hard. I want you to know that I'm gonna love your son like he's my own, and I will never abandon him. Ever." I shake my head. "I miss you, man. Tell mamma I miss her too. I'll see you again soon."

I stand up, wipe the back of my pants off and walk into the living room. I sit on the sofa next to Asia, she lays her head in my lap and I stroke her hair. After getting shot, Asia lost a lot of blood, and almost didn't make it. I was tripped out when I found out we shared the same blood type, I told them to drain me until I died if it meant saving her life. She took a bullet to her ribs but she survived, and we were both enrolled in school for the next semester. My bitch a gangster.

"Your tummy hurt," she asks me. "You were in the bathroom for awhile. What you was doing, taking a shit?"

"Yeah, but I'm cool now." I rub her warm cheek. "How you feeling?"

"Dane, when you gonna stop asking me how I'm doing? It's been months since I've been shot. You need to relax, baby."

"I'm never going to not ask you how you feel, Asia."

She smiles. "Well...how are you doing? I mean how are you really doing, since your brother has been gone? And your mother."

"I don't know how to feel." I don't tell her about the conversation I had earlier in the bathroom with my brother, because she'll want me to elaborate, and I don't feel like talking. Me and my mother never had a relationship, because she was always mentally gone.

"The only thing I'm worried about right now is you and my nephew. So let's focus on us, deal?"

She raises her head and kisses me gently on the lips. "Deal."

EPILOGUE

Dane was sitting on the bench on the campus. Two beautiful college girls were on the left and right of him.

"Dane, how come your eyes so pretty," the redbone asked him. "You got contacts in or something? 'Cause I ain't never seen eyes as nice as yours before." Dane had laser surgery so the contacts were no longer needed.

Dane moved his face so close to hers, their lips almost touched. "Can you see my eyes? Real good?"

Her heart palpitated being so close to him. She wanted him so badly she could taste him, only if he let her. "Yeah...uh...what you want me to see by looking into your eyes?"

"You see any contact lenses lines in my eyes," he asked softly.

"No," she giggled. "I don't see nothing but emerald."

He moved his head away. "Well that answered your question. Everything on me real, ma."

Before she could respond, the cute brown skin girl turned his head so that he was looking into her eyes. "That hasn't answered my question." She moved her face so close to his, their lips brushed. "Oh...you right, them eyes are all yours." She ran her hand up his thigh and toward his stiffening dick. Women were forever his weakness. "And this dick is yours too. When you gonna dump that girlfriend of yours, and get with me?"

Dane immediately grew angry, and moved his face away from hers. "Aight then, it's time to go. I'm kinda busy."

Cute Brown skin snatched her hand away. "Why you acting all funny all of a sudden? If you acted right tonight, we were going to hook you up, and give you that threesome we talked about in Calculus class."

"It ain't about acting funny, it's about me wanting to study before my next class. Now I'll appreciate if you two bounce."

Light skin girl giggled. "It's cool, we know you one minute away from marriage. Well, your girlfriend is lucky to have your loyal ass." She looked at her friend. "For now anyway. Come on girl"— she grabbed her friend's hand— "let's get out of here, before the nigga starts crying."

When both of them left, Asia walked over to her man and sat in his lap. She saw the entire scene play out, and her heart broke because she knew there was no controlling him. Pushing him too much would force him backwards in their relationship, but letting him roam too freely could get him snatched.

"How's your day, baby?" she wrapped her arms around his neck. "

"Good," he looked into her eyes and squeezed her ass cheek. After all the years they'd been together, she was still beautiful. "What about yours?"

"It was okay, until I remembered something."

"Aw, shit, what did you remember, Asia?" he chuckled. "Let me gear myself up for this."

"For starters I'm gonna start axing these bitches at this school, if they keep overstepping their boundaries. I mean why they gotta push up on you, when they know we together? It ain't like we don't walk up and down the school halls arm in arm. You're mine, Dane."

"College halls."

"I'm serious, Dane! I'm getting sick of this shit. They make me want to pop your pretty green eyes out of your head, forcing them to be creative and think of another topic to try and rope you."

He laughed, and covered his eyes. She hit his hands and they dropped in his lap. "Look, you're my baby, Asia. And yes, I probably flirt too much with these bitches 'round here, which I'm gonna work on, but I just want you to know that you belong to me. There ain't shit they can do to get me to leave you, and believe me they've tried."

"Then prove it."

"Okay, how you want me to prove it?"

Asia got up, dropped on her knee and pulled out a ring box in her pocket. "What you doing, baby?" Dane asked looking around.

"Dane Blake"—she continues ignoring him— "I have loved you for all of my life. From the moment you sent me a weed plant for Valentine's Day, and told me I belong to you. I took that seriously, baby, and even took a bullet in my side to prove my love and never mentioned it again before today, because I wanted it to count. So I'm asking you, will you do me the honor, of being my husband?"

He focuses on her beautiful chocolate skin, her big pretty eyes, and her over all style. Every time a chick stepped to him, he would compare them to her and be turned off when they fell short and didn't measure up. He was starting to believe that his plight to always have a bevvy of women on his roster was his unconscious way of never wanting to be alone. But with her, he wouldn't have to be.

And then there was the other thing hovering over his head. Memory, the bitch he fucked on the side awhile back, found out what college he was enrolled in, and told his counselor that it was important that she gave him her number, because the old one he had changed. When he called Memory he learned that she was pregnant and was keeping the baby. The worst thing? She wanted him to step up and be a father. If he married Asia, he would never have to worry about losing her once she found out about the child, or so he thought.

He swallowed and said, "Yes."

Her smile brightened. "Yes what?"

"Yes I'll marry you."

She slid the ring on his finger, hopped up and jumped into his lap. She planted soft kisses all around his neck and face, reached into her pocket and handed him a nickel bag of weed. "I'm gonna do you so good, Dane. You'll see."

"I already know, ma," he chuckled. "I know you got me."

While they were in a world of their own, Da Chun was sitting in the bench on the other side of the campus. The driver's cap was no longer on her head, and her natural hair was dressed in two pig-tails. She looked just like a college student.

She removed her phone from her pocket and said, "Mercury, they're here. What you want me to do?"

"You see the girl?"

Filled with jealousy she said, "Yes, she's here too." She knew where his intentions lied when in came to Asia, and she hated it.

"Don't do anything, I'm on my way. Just keep them in your sights."

THE CARTEL PUBLICATIONS

"We Reign Supreme"

A NOVEL BY

REIGN

CARTEL PUBLICATIONS
PRESENTS

FIRST
COMES
Love
THEN COMES
MURDER

YOUNG AND

DUMB

DUCK SANCHEZ

CARTEL PUBLICATIONS

PRESENTS

The Cartel Collection
Established in January 2008
We're growing stronger by the month!!!
www.thecartelpublications.com

Cartel Publications Order Form
Inmates ONLY get novels for $10.00 per book!

Titles	_Fee_
Shyt List	$15.00
Shyt List 2	$15.00
Pitbulls In A Skirt	$15.00
Pitbulls In A Skirt 2	$15.00
Pitbulls In A Skirt 3	$15.00
Pitbulls In A Skirt 4	$15.00
Victoria's Secret	$15.00
Poison	$15.00
Poison 2	$15.00
Hell Razor Honeys	$15.00
Hell Razor Honeys 2	$15.00
A Hustler's Son 2	$15.00
Black And Ugly As Ever	$15.00
Year of The Crack Mom	$15.00
The Face That Launched a Thousand Bullets	
	$15.00
The Unusual Suspects	$15.00
Miss Wayne & The Queens of DC	
	$15.00
Year of The Crack Mom	$15.00
Familia Divided	$15.00
Shyt List III	$15.00
Shyt List IV	$15.00
Raunchy	$15.00
Raunchy 2	$15.00
Raunchy 3	$15.00
Reversed	$15.00
Quita's Dayscare Center	$15.00
Quita's Dayscare Center 2	$15.00
Shyt List V	$15.00
Deadheads	$15.00
Pretty Kings	$15.00
Drunk & Hot Girls	$15.00
Hersband Material	$15.00
Upscale Kittens	$15.00
Wake & Bake Boys	$15.00

Please add $4.00 **per book for shipping and handling.**
The Cartel Publications * P.O. Box 486 * Owings Mills * MD * 21117

Name: _____

Address:_____

City/State:_____

Contact # & Email:_____

Please allow 5-7 business days for delivery. The Cartel is not
responsible for prison orders rejected.

Personal Checks Are Not Accepted.

24795530R00117

Made in the USA
Lexington, KY
01 August 2013